MURDER
SHE SPOKE

Other books and e-books by Robin Wood:
"Only the Raven Knows"
"Perpetrator of Hidden Notes"
"Harley's Babe"
"Trouble Follows Kids and Dogs"
"Battling Lodges"
"Ready-Aim-Fire"
"Driving Her Crazy"

I would like to hear from any reader. Write to author:
Robin Wood, P.O. Box 1125, Concrete, WA 98237

Rev. date: 05/16/2014

To order additional copies of this book, contact:
Xlibris LLC
1-888-795-4274
www.Xlibris.com
Orders@Xlibris.com
611160

Dear Reader,

This was the hardest book I have tried to write. Can you imagine correcting a novel where you have to read about gory details time and time again? I wish I could just go throw-up behind a bush. I wish I could just spell things correctly the first time around.

Next you had to keep writing clues down even if you never used them again. Real mystery writers probably just do this by rote.

Then you get sick and nearly forget what you were writing about. Oh, woe is me!

Enough of that, I had so much help on this book, that I really only wrote it by the incidents I was told about. Of course; change the names to protect the innocent, make the incident into fiction by your own words and hope it turns out a little funny even if is not funny, but tragic. I owe a debit of gratitude to those who helped me with their stories. Policemen and policewomen do not like to talk about their jobs, just like servicemen do not talk about what they do. However, truck drivers are a field of information.

Thank you all.

I hope you readers like the story.

Sincerely,
Robin Wood

Many thanks go to those I was fortunate enough to get to interview for help with this book. I needed it. I hope I didn't make too many mistakes and if I did: Readers, they are all mine.

Lt. R.G. Feederle, retired LAPD

Diane Tanguy, retired Alaska Fish and Wildlife

Randy Wood, long haul truck driver

"River" lady truck driver

Martha Johnson

Carol Fabrick

Upper Skagit Writers Group

Robin's picture was

Provided by

The Cocrete Herald

MURDER
SHE SPOKE

I hope you enjoy
the book

Robin Wood

ROBIN WOOD

2017

This novel is dedicated to my friends:

MARTHA JOHNSON and her son,

ALLEN LEE

And my best friend

NANCY COOK

Who introduced me to Martha

Two of the nicest women you'll ever meet.

ON AND OFF THE BEAT #1

The ringing of the telephone echoed through the empty apartment. On the fifth ring the answering machine kicked in.

A frantic voice speaks with a slight accent, *"If you're there, Laryn, please pickup the phone. He's so mad he says he's going to kill me."* A pause ensues. *"Oh no! Please no!" screamed the voice. A scuffle and a thud are recorded.* After a few minutes the phone is hung up. The answering machine clicks off.

Laryn Scott trudged tiredly up the stairs to her second floor apartment overlooking the Skagit River. It was always a pleasure, rain or shine, to get home, pour a glass of wine and looked out her nook's window at the river. Its flow drew the tiredness out of her, draining the day's troubles away like it drained the Skagit Valley of excess water in good old Washington State.

Unlocking her door at the top of the stairs, she entered her apartment *to* a blaze of light shining in from the setting sun. It was hard to see the blinking red light on her answering machine. From habit, she hit the playback button, slapped her mail on the retro 50's table, grabbed a glass from the cupboard and was pouring her glass of wine when the word 'Laryn' caught her attention.

She put the wine bottle back in the refrigerator, set her glass on the table next to her mail and went over to hit the playback button. Her heart was beating frantically at what she thought she had heard. Numerous messages had to play back first. Why, oh why, couldn't they make a machine that you could just play whatever message you wanted to hear. She felt like hitting the button again just to speed it on its way, which wouldn't work, or crash it to the floor which would break the darn thing.

Delete! Delete! Hurry up! Hurry up! Finally *the* message she wanted *to* hear.

"*If you're there, Laryn, please pick up the phone. He's so mad, he says he going to kill me.*" Pause. "*Oh no! Please no!*" A scuffle, a thud and then you could hear the click of the phone cutting off the open line.

She hit the playback button again. Getting out her cell phone, she readied it to copy the frantic call. Who's getting killed? Darn it, did everyone who called think she knew who they *were* by just their voice? *All* these thoughts went through her head as *she* waited.

The few calls she had to save she listened to again, then the call she wanted to hear came back on and she copied the frantic message. Acting like the cop she was, she quickly called the Mount Vernon precinct.

Harve answered from the front desk.

"Hi, Harve, this is Laryn. I've just listened to a frantic call from a woman asking for my help. She thought she was going to be murdered. Has anyone called the precinct?"

"*Funny you should ask, Laryn, calls are coming in from all over about a woman's call. No name mentioned. Even the fire department was called, but not a single call to 911.*" Harve continued, "*Did the lady say she was being killed?*"

"Yes, she did," replied Laryn. "I taped her call on my cell phone. Would you like to hear it?"

"*Sure, come down to the precinct and we'll listen to both of the calls. Maybe we'll get a hint on who made this call.*"

"Okay, I'll be right down." It was strange, thought Laryn, you could be so tired you could sleep on rocks, but an emergency would feed the body to full alertness.

Since she was still fully dressed, she grabbed her car keys and headed out to her car. As she drove, she went over in her mind of all the women she knew who had a slight accent and would call her by her given name. Their voices and names clicked through her brain like a computer call-up.

That voice on the answering machine could have been anyone, but Laryn's mind was pulling out two names that matched the slightly accented voice she had heard. It was emergencies like this that reinforced her belief that she'd make a darned good detective if given the chance.

She'd gone to Mount Vernon's schools, plus had played sports with many other schools girl's teams. She had a huge repertoier of voices and names to think about and try to match. She'd do some more thinking about names and voices, but to start with, she'd go with the two names that stuck out at her right now.

Meanwhile, maybe the patrol cars would have run into the trouble that might have just happened.

She pulled into the precinct. Inside, the waiting room wasn't busy. Harve, at the desk, didn't seem all that concerned. Here she was ballistic and everyone else was just going about their business. Harve was a good-old-guy; nearly ready for retirement, bald and running to belly fat, but was always sunny and bright.

Harve looked up at the tall, statuesque blond with a boy-like haircut. She was a newly rising star in her job; quick-witted and smart. "How you doin', Laryn?"

"Not so good, Harve. My heart's beating pretty wildly. Where's that message I need to hear?"

"Over here, girl." He got up to open the half-door kept lock at all times. You would have to jump over it to get to Harve's side. Laryn went through and turned back to the phones. Here the system was different than the one at her house. You could send a message to another phone to be saved. She pulled up a rolling chair and sat down as she pushed the button to hear the message.

The slightly accented voice came on, *"Isn't anyone around? I need help. He said when he got here, he was going to kill me for sure. I'm calling Laryn next."*

Harve listened with her. "Is that the voice you heard on your phone?"

She looked up at him. "I think so. It has the same slight accent and it sounds like a woman. Here, listen to what I recorded on my cell phone."

Laryn and Harve listened to her playback.

"I agree, Laryn. It does sound like the recording here at the station, only that one sounds like whatever was going to happen, just did. That's scary." He shook his head in denial. "What's your take on this?"

Laryn pursed her mouth. "I've been going over in my mind of all the girls I have known. My mind keeps coming up with two names. I'll call those women right now if I can find them."

She looked up Estelle Baronia's number. Estelle's mother answered.

"Mrs. Baronia, This is Laryn Scott. I'm calling to talk to Estelle."

"Hello, Laryn. Estelle doesn't live here any more. She and Bonnie got an apartment together. They both work at the same place, so they can commute together and share the rent."

"Do you think she could be home from work now?"

"No. It is my understanding she took a trip with her boyfriend to Disneyland in California. She should be back in a week."

"Thank you, Mrs. Baronia. I'll check back with her after she gets back. Can I have her phone number?"

Mrs. Baronia knew her, so gave Laryn the number. She carefully wrote the number down and who it was for and pertaining to what. You carefully recorded all your conversations, time, dates. It was part of her job.

Harve had left her alone and was back at his place at the desk. Laryn looked up her next number. It was to Feliz Toreno. She got the answering machine. She left a message. "Mr. Toreno, this is Laryn Scott. I'm calling for Maya. Is she home? Please call me back at my cell phone number." She gave him the number and hung up.

"Harve, my women are not available right now. I might as well go back home." She leaned over his desk. "Will you call me if there is any update on this case?"

Harve looked up at her. "So, you think this might be a case?"

"I hope not, but sad to say, I do think something is wrong. It's those bad feelings you get before you enter a suspected crime scene and it turns out to really be a crime scene."

Harve shook his head. "Yeah, I do know what you mean. Man, I am so glad I'm almost retired. Each one of those incidents took years off my life."

Laryn smiled at him. "You can tell I'm new to this game. I still get an adrenaline rush, but not this time." She sobered quickly. She slapped her hand on his deck. "I'm off."

Not tired or hungry anymore, she decided to stop off at the Health Club and work off a little steam. She grinned to herself. She wouldn't mind seeing Quinn Madden, again. Man, that dude had muscles up the 'ying-yang.' It made her eyes water at the beauty of those muscles lifting and flexing. It raised her heart beat, too. Wasn't that what the workouts were supposed to do? Yeah, raise her heartbeat. She shook her head in time to the music playing on her car's radio.

She parked and locked her car, then went in the Health Club. Quinn wasn't on the desk, but she could see him working with a person on one of the weight benches. He had shorts on and a sleeveless muscle-shirt, his pony tail holding his curly, dark brown hair back from his neck.

She took a stair-climber where she could watch the muscles of the weight lifters. A little workout and a lot of watching would get her heart rate up better than a good run.

Her legs pumped up—down—up—down. Heart rate:—pitter—patter—pitter—patter.

"Hey, pretty lady, what's up?"

Heart rate—plop! Legs stopped.

Laryn almost choked on her saliva, "Hi, yourself. Quinn. I see you've been working the field of muscle-bound men. Can't you find something better to do?" She eyed his hair where the curls clung to his forehead framing a strong face.

"Yeah, I just did. When did you come in?" He jumped on the stair-climber beside her.

"Just a few minutes ago, I had some excess energy I needed to get rid of."

He grinned at her. "That must have been what I felt. All of a sudden there was this surge of energy invigorating the room. My head jerked up— and there you were. What's up?"

"How do you know anything is up? I come in here all the time."

"Sure you do, but not at this time of night. You should be home eating or just relaxing. You usually come in here later or early in the morning before work."

"Man, you sure do have my schedule down pat."

"Hey, not many beautiful women come in here. I think the pretty women are afraid of sweating. They don't come here to work out, they come here to check out the bodies. They bike a little, but that's about all"

Caught up by her, womanly wiles, "How do you know that's not what I'm doing?"

He chuckled. "Because you really do get a sweat up and work all our machines."

Yeah, well, she was sweating right now and the machine wasn't even working. He might not know it, but his leg muscles bunched up and then straightened out. Up—down—up—down. Good Lord she was hyperventilating and sweating. She had a fixation on muscles.

Maybe, she should fixate on his eyes. Oh my God, they were as blue as the sky on a nice day, blue as the irises blooming in May, blue as lupines along the highway.

She changed thoughts. "I'll have you know people don't sweat, we perspire. Horses sweat"

He laughed, "Could be, but it doesn't sound right to say, 'I'm going to break perspiration' instead of 'I'm going to break sweat' or 'no perspiration' instead of 'no sweat' meaning 'no problem.'"

She grinned at him, "I see your point. Okay, Quinn Madden. Will you go harass some other person? I need to get my legs moving again."

He laughed at her as he stepped down from the step-climber. "Remember to shower, Laryn Scott, before you leave. You're sweating rather profusely."

Ugh! "Gee, thanks a lot for those profound words. Makes a girl feel real special to be able to sweat to your high standards." She watched that tight butt walk away from her. She hoped he couldn't feel her eyes boring into his back side. His laugh told her he did.

Quinn smiled as he left Laryn to her workout. He liked harassing her. She always had a quick comeback and was comfortable within her own body, too. He liked that. She was tall for a woman and cut her blonde hair like a businessman. It looked good on her and didn't detract from her lovely face.

He looked around to see who he hadn't welcomed. Being the manager of an athletic club made him interact with people when he'd rather just stay behind the scenes. Aw, there was another overweight man he could offer advice on how to exercise without straining their muscles or causing a heart attack. He headed that way.

Laryn made it back home to her apartment, but the sun was down and only by opening the sliders to her small deck could she enjoy the sounds and smells of the Skagit River. And now, that she was back home again, the mystery of the phone call came back to plague her.

She had picked up a hamburger and fries with a large coke at a drive-through, so flipped on the TV and ate her quickie-meal. When she was finished, she cleaned up her greasy paper mess, while still watching the TV show.

The phone rang. Still keeping her eye on the TV show, she absentmindedly answered, "Laryn Scott, how may I help you?"

"Miz Scott, this is Feliz Toreno. I got your message."

"Mr. Toreno, I called about Maya. Is she home?"

"No, she tells me she is going on a trip with her boyfriend. She is gone, so must have left this morning."

"A trip, huh? When do you think she'll be back?"

"She don't tell me, she just say to me, when her fellow comes to town, she will go on a trip with him. She works at truck-stop café, maybe the café will know more than her poor old papa."

"Did she say who the fellow was or what he does when he comes to town?"

"No name, but he's a truck driver. I had alfalfa delivered today, but I don't know if that was her boyfriend or not."

"Do you know the alfalfa truck driver's name?

"No. He left invoice copy, but the name is scribble. All I care is I got alfalfa."

"If Maya comes back or calls you, could you let me know? Someone called me today, but didn't leave their number or name. I'm just trying to call them back to see what they wanted me for."

"Yes, I will Miz Scott."

They hung up. Darn, she needed to upgrade her phone to caller I.D., but would her old retro phone accept caller I.D.? She'd have to find out.

Laryn's program was over and she hadn't seen the ending. How many times did she miss endings of TV shows? Man, another thing she needed was to get one of those things so you could tape your show to watch later. However, she never had time later either, so maybe the next time it was re-run she'd just watch the ending and forget the rest of the program.

———

She turned the TV off, checked the locks on her door and got ready for bed. She made a note in her head to check at the café where Maya worked to see what they knew about the trip or the truck driver Maya might be with. Darn, both of her suspects were on vacation.

She needed to think about voices of other women she knew. She shouldn't just suspect these two out of the hundred others she'd been in contact with. Now, like a dog with a bone, she'd worry it to death. She scratched her head. Poor choice of words: *death*.

ON AND OFF THE BEAT #2

It was her regular day at work. Laryn cruised around Mount Vernon for awhile. Stopped near the high school to make sure no one was speeding away from the school, kidnapped, or maybe dealing drugs and a million other things that went subconsciously through a cop's mind when they were on duty.

It was a beautiful day, made more beautiful by no troubles brewing. Nearing supper time, she decided to go to the truck stop for a salad and coffee. She parked the cruiser towards the back so it wouldn't seem like something was going on there to make people shy away from trouble.

Inside she took a seat near the back so she could watch the door. Laryn laughed at herself. This was the old gun fighter syndrome; keep your back to the wall and your face to the door. She wasn't anticipating a problem. She just wanted a little information and food.

Her waitress came up. "Hi! My name is Shirley. I'll be your waitress for tonight. How may I help you?"

Laryn responded. "I'd like a cup of coffee and your chef salad, please."

Shirley wrote it into her pad and nodded. "Thank you. That will be coming right up."

Laryn watched her walk away to deliver her order to the chef. When Shirley came back maybe she could answer a few questions. She looked around. There were quite a few truck drivers eating and laughing together. She knew they didn't have to know one another to get a conversation going. It was the brotherhood of truckers to make friends with other truckers wherever they went.

Her salad arrived with Shirley and the coffeepot. The coffee was poured.

"Is there anything else I can do for you?" asked Shirley.

Laryn looked up at her. "Do you know Maya Toreno?"

"Not really. I'm taking her place for the next few weeks until she gets back. I was on another shift when I was asked to take this one. Is anything wrong?"

Laryn smiled, "Not really, she's an old friend of mine. Where did she go?"

Shirley shrugged her shoulders. "It's rumored she went on vacation with her trucker boyfriend. They expect her back in a week or so." She leaned into Laryn, "Even on my shift, its rumored she's acting like a tramp with the guy." Shirley rolled her eyes.

"Do you know his name?"

Shirley shook her head. "There's so many of them." She swung her arm out to encompass everyone in the room.

Laryn grimaced, "Thanks Shirley. I'll stop by another day to see her."

Shirley poured coffee before she went back to her station.

Laryn finished her salad and headed back to the precinct. Her day was over and she could report it as a good one since nothing happened on her shift.

When she got back to her apartment, the answering machine was blinking. Alert to it now, she rushed over to listen to it before she did anything.

It was just her mother. *"Laryn dear, we're having a fried chicken supper tomorrow night. I hope you can come. Your brother will be here with a friend."*

Oh great! Her mother was setting her up with another friend. This time it was her brother's. When would they all get it through their heads that she didn't need a man in her life? She had a whole precinct full of men; married, single and weird. There were a few women, too, but it seemed they were never on the same shift as she was, so they only met in the locker room between shifts.

Now, if any of her cohorts would have a friend like Quinn Madden at the Health Club, she might be interested. He didn't strike her as a macho-man even if he was muy-macho in build. He seemed to talk to everyone and laughed and slapped them on the back or hand squeezed their shoulders for a job well done. He even watched to see if they were drinking enough water and would bring a bottle around if he felt they needed it. Not to mention he was good looking, too.

She poured her glass of wine and sat down at her retro 50's table with its chrome tubular legs and gray Formica top. Her chairs were in a bright yellow vinyl. It cheered her up just to be home. Her ceramic glass stared back at her with a girl's face, bright red lips and flame red hair emblazoned on it. She could even talk to her glass and not feel that she was talking to an empty room. Looking out on the Skagit River as it flowed toward Puget Sound bay, she reveled in her good fortune to have found this apartment and have a job she felt worthy of.

Her old cat-clock, with its rolling eyes and its swinging tail, struck the hour. It was time to watch her few favorite shows and the news, then to bed. Another day, another dollar.

Laryn had worked her shift without any problems. Man, two days in a row without an incident. It made you feel good, but also, worried you that it was stacking up to a big blow-up and tomorrow was her mother's Sunday dinner.

The next morning, she showered and changed into an ankle length, cream colored skirt with a pink flowered blouse. She thought her knee-high tan boots went well with it. Her mother liked her to show up looking like a girl and not the tomboy she grew up as.

With a brother not much older and an uncle that led her and her brother into more scrapes than her mother even knew about made it hard to be a prissy girl. Being tall, made the fellows forget she was a girl and creaming them at basketball had helped her image as a tomboy.

She took the curling iron to her front bangs that normally were combed back and jelled into place. Now they framed her forehead. The *piece de resistance* were her long dangly, butterfly earrings camouflaging her long neck. There! She defied her mother telling her she wasn't dressing feminine enough.

Grabbing a light jacket and her car keys, out the door she went automatically locking it.

She arrived just in time according to her watch. The family house was up on the hill in Mount Vernon. The neighbors kept their yards mowed and flowers blooming. It looked beautiful, but she was glad she didn't have to help keep things up any more. Her only flowers were silk ones in a vase and her green stuff was an ivy plant she just had to water. Her mother didn't think she was a prissy girl when it came to mowing and weeding. In that aspect, she and her brother were equals. Go figure!

She went in the house without knocking since she was expected. "Hi, Mom, I'm home."

Her mother came out of the kitchen where the aroma of frying chicken wafted on the air. "Just in time, I see, and my but you look nice." Her mother came over and kissed her on the cheek. "You smell nice, too."

"Thanks, Mom. Is Dayne here yet?"

"No, he'll be here when the chicken smell permeates as far as the school gym."

Laryn nodded. Her brother still lived at home even though he taught school and was an assistant football coach. He didn't care to have a quiet place of his own and her mother and father didn't object. In fact, when they went on vacation, the house was occupied.

Her brother wasn't a person who took advantage of his parents. He did his own washing, cooked meals when he had a day off, mowed the lawn, took out garbage and seemed to have a set list of things he would do without being asked.

She was glad her mother had someone else to look after and to hook-up for dates. Dayne hated it as much as she did. At least, if she or Dayne ever did get married and have kids, they wouldn't have to worry about a babysitter.

She followed her mother into the kitchen. "Shall I set the table?"

"I did some of it already. You could get the salt and pepper and butter on the table. I've made biscuits that I just have to put in the oven at the last minute. If you'd like some of that wonderful wild blackberry jam your dad makes, put it in a nice dish with a small spoon will you, please."

Laryn went about doing the last minute things. It was what she normally did when she came to dinner. The menu might change, but the things that went on the dinner table did not.

She'd just finished her part of the dinner preparations when her brother burst in the door. She leaned her head into the kitchen.

"The dog smelled the bone. Dayne's here."

Her mother came out of the kitchen to greet her son and his guest. Laryn followed.

Dayne grabbed his mother in a hug. "Hi, Mom." He turned to his friend. "Meet my friend and co-worker, Quinn Madden. Quinn this is my mom, Samantha Scott. Mom's an author of romantic fiction. Beware of her interrogation."

Quinn nodded. "I'm glad to meet you, Mrs. Scott. The smell of that chicken is making my knees weak."

Samantha shook his hand with her face flaming a deep red. "Oh go on with you. It's just a simple fried chicken dinner for the family." She spread her hand wide and motioned, "Go sit down. Can I get you boys anything to drink?"

"I'll get it, Mom." Without asking what Quinn might want Dayne left to get them something cold.

Laryn stood there with her mouth open. Her brother's friend was the hunk from the Health Club. How did he meet up with her brother? Her brother only had dorky friends and he wouldn't think of introducing them to her. Not that he thought she was a nerd. He just realized that their mother did enough of the match-making to last them both into the next century. His friends were his and her friends were hers.

Quinn was certainly dressed nicely. His white shirt with military creases was fresh from the cleaners. His slacks were pressed within a micro-inch of a cutting edge. He still had his ponytail slicked back with those cute escaped curls near his forehead and that gold necklace around his masculine neck. Laryn had to slurp back the drool from dripping down her chin.

Samantha eyed the two standing there. "Laryn, your brother didn't think to introduce you to Quinn." She looked at Quinn, "This is Dayne's sister, Laryn. She works for the Mount Vernon police department."

Quinn smiled a bright smile and winked at her. "Oh, I know Laryn. I just didn't realize we knew anyone in common." He turned to Laryn's mother. "I know her from the Athletic Club. She stops by whenever she can to work out." He grinned at Laryn, "She sweats a lot." He looked her up and down, "But I must say, she cleans up real good."

Laryn held out her hand to shake Quinn's. If she had been alone, she'd have punched him out. She'd show him. As he took her hand, she leaned in for a hug. Let him smell her man-getting perfume. For a change, she was glad her mother insisted on her acting, smelling and looking like a girl.

Oh, oh! She forgot he might have his women-getting shaving lotion on. He smelled like something from the southseas. Her knees felt weak again.

"I'm glad to formally be introduced to you. My brother usually brings home dogs, but you're at least a change."

Quinn looked a little confused. "Dogs, huh?"

Dayne came back into the living room. He had two cold drinks with him. "Here's a Pepsi. If you'd like some booze in it, I can get some."

Quinn took the drink. "No, this is fine." He looked up at Dayne. "I didn't know you collected dogs. Do you run a kennel besides teaching and coaching football?"

To Laryn, Dayne did his usual dumb look. For a smart fellow, she felt he was her dumb brother. He could talk but he didn't understand jokes unless he told them. It might be that Quinn wasn't much better.

"Run a kennel? Why would you think I run a kennel?"

Laryn grinned at Quinn. "Yeah, why do you think he'd run a kennel?"

Quinn made a face, "Because you said he brought dogs home. I get the message. You don't think I'm a dog, but I'm probably coming in on close to that now, huh!"

Laryn cocked her head at him, "If the shoe fits you get to wear it."

Quinn smiled back, "Can I at least be a bulldog?"

Dayne punched his sister's shoulder lightly, otherwise she'd retaliate back with a shove. "If this is the way you're going to treat my friends, I won't let you meet any more of them."

Laryn punched him back lightly, "One's enough, brother dear."

Quinn looked concerned. "Shall I go home? I don't want to start a dog and cat fight especially before I get to eat home fried chicken."

Laryn and Dayne turned back to him. It was like looking at twins. Both were tall and blond. Both had a chagrinned look on their faces. They stammered and said, "I'm sorry! Don't go!"

Quinn laughed. "Okay, now I see the resemblance. It's like looking at two parrots and they 'squawk!'."

Again, the two parroted, "Squawk?"

He nodded, "Yep, squawk."

Samantha came back into the room saving the whole situation by announcing, "Dinner is ready. Wash up and take a seat."

ON AND OFF THE BEAT #3

Dinner had gone the way of a gigantic garbage disposal. The fellows had eaten like they had never tasted anything so good. Laryn thought maybe Quinn hadn't had a meal like her mother cooked in a long time. Her brother was different. He ate like that all the time. He didn't gain weight because he was so active.

She, on the other hand, had to work out and watch what she ate. Her job wasn't that active just riding around in a patrol car, but she had to qualify once a year to keep her job.

She thought of the table conversations. Her brother had asked Quinn to help him get the football team in shape. Quinn had volunteered his time to teach them nutrition and weight training.

Not to be outdone, she had volunteered to teach them all how to shoot a pistol and, boy, did that get a raise out of her family. She only wanted to get a little attention even though she knew that was childish.

She went home early.

Laryn changed out of her dressy clothes and into her T-shirt sporting the saying, *can you run faster than a speeding bullet* and her sleep-in shorts. She plopped down on her dark blue bedspread with wild colorful swirls on it to remove her stockings. Here she always felt like she was in the galaxy when she lay under it. She pulled back the bedspread and crawled under the blankets. Come to me, Captain Kirk or Spock, ran through her head as she went to sleep.

The next morning came early. Laryn took her shower before her coffee. The coffee tasted better when she was awake. Her Clint Eastwood coffee cup said 'Make my day'. It put her in the right mood for her police officer's duties. She didn't have to be at work until noon. This meant she would work later into the evening. It didn't matter.

She started her run. She loved to run this early, when the sky was just breaking light, the birds started to sing and most dogs were still inside with their masters or mistresses. Sometimes when it was raining she would lift her face to the spatters and let her cares wash away. Dress for the weather was the secret.

Her thoughts wandered to the night before when she was at dinner and the surprise for the evening was Quinn as the other guest. Her folks even liked him. Some of the friends her brother brought home were a mess. He really did bring home *dogs* that needed care. He would mentor fellows to try to change their ways and his thoughts were a good meal cooked by their mother was a good start.

He wanted to show them what a real home was like and maybe someday they would model their home after his folk's. He was a good guy, but just didn't realize some people didn't want to be saved, but would take a good, free meal if offered one.

She looked around. An older couple lived up ahead in a cozy cottage. You could tell time by Mr. Osmund. He usually came out to get his paper about now and they each gave a cordial good morning to each other. He wasn't outdoors yet. Strange!

Could something have happened to the older couple? Laryn was trained to look out for signs like this. Her woman's intuition said something was wrong. No sign of life and no lights were on in the house either. She jogged in place for a minute.

A person in a hooded sweatshirt peeked out from around a bush beside the house. When he saw her took off running.

Crapolla, now she had to chase him down. The jerk didn't know she had been a track star.

Laryn yelled at the suspect. "Halt or I'll shoot!"

The suspect just ran faster. Oh well, she thought, sometimes that worked.

She dialed 911 as she ran. Her morning was ruined. Her thoughts were flying through her head. She hoped the older couple was all right.

"911, what's your emergency?"

"This is Officer Laryn Scott. Please send a squad car to this street." She flashed a picture of the street sign. "I'm chasing a person in a suspected home invasion."

Just then she caught up with the perpetrator. Laryn grabbed the person's sweatshirt by the hood and threw him to the ground. He was a skinny little punk, so she sat on him. He squirreled around, but couldn't move much or do any damage to her. She still had her phone on with the 911 operator.

"I have him down. Are my guys coming?"

"Yes. Stay on the line until they show up."

The perp beat his hands on the ground, "I didn't do nothin'."

"Then why did you run?"

"Because you were chasing me."

"I didn't chase you until you ran."

"Who the hell are you, lady? You are a lady aren't you?"

Laryn did an extra push down on him for that smart remark. "Can't you tell? I don't have a boney butt like most men?"

Just then a squad car pulled up.

An officer jumped out. "What's going on, Officer Scott?"

"I'm not sure. Can we take this guy into custody until we check out the home of the Osmunds'? I'm hoping they are all right."

"You can't arrest me. I didn't do nothin' to those old people. And if I did, they asked for it."

Officer Brumell looked at Laryn and raised his eyebrows. He quickly cuffed the guy, read him his Miranda Rights and stuffed him into the squad car. The suspect cussed and scream *police brutality* at them.

Laryn opened the other door and crawled in the shotgun seat. "It's just up the street. I was on my morning jog, when something felt wrong at the Osmunds. Then this fellow poked his head around a bush and when he saw me, he took off running. I caught him right after he crossed the street."

"Yeah, and you wouldn't have if I hadn't tripped."

Laryn turned to face him. "You didn't trip, punk, I pulled you to the ground."

The little creep yelled, "Yeah and that's why I called *police brutality*."

Since it was less than a half a block to the Osmunds, the squad car pulled up. The neighborhood was quiet as a tomb. That was what had worried Laryn. Since she was off-duty, she stayed in the squad car with the prisoner. Officer Brumell went to the door and knock. No answer. He went around to the back door. Here Laryn lost track of him. She worried. The Osmunds were a nice couple and she wished them good health.

Soon, Officer Brumell came to the front door. He was talking on his cell phone. Reaching the squad car, he leaned into Laryn's window she had opened so she could hear anything that might be going on.

"I've called for an ambulance. Mr. Osmund was hit on the head, but says he feels all right. He's going to check on his wife who had locked herself in the bathroom, but with no phone. I've called for backup."

"I didn't hit him. He fell when he tried to pull the sack away from me."

Laryn raised her eyebrows. "What sack was that?"

"I ain't got no sack."

Officer Brumell left to check on the man and his wife. At their age, either one could have a heart attack. Laryn could hear the ambulance coming and maybe more squad cars. She shook her head. It was a lot of noise anyway for this time of the morning. Here she was just enjoying a morning run and now she had the whole neighborhood being awakened very soon. She threw up her hands. Yeah like right now.

Lights were coming on in houses. The ambulance pulled up and the medics quickly went about their business. Another squad car pulled up. This let Laryn off the hook for the prisoner so she could go check on the elderly couple.

She rushed into the house. The medics were checking the vitals of the couple.

The elderly man looked up, "Thanks, Miss Scott. I'm glad you were out jogging this morning. When I came out of the bedroom to go get the paper, there was a young fellow going though our things. When I grabbed the sack he was putting things in, he pushed me and I fell backwards and hit my head on the door casing. My wife heard the commotion and rushed into the bathroom where she could lock the door."

Laryn nodded her head. "Did he leave the sack here?"

The medic looked at Laryn. "I'm sorry but we need to transport Mr. Osmund to the hospital for observation."

The medic elbowed Laryn out of the way. She backed up until they had him loaded on the gurney.

Mr. Osmund leaned his head forward. "I don't see the sack right here, but I've not had time to look around for it."

"That's all right, Mr. Osmund. I think I know where to look." She followed the medics and the gurney out the door. "Take care, Mr. Osmund. I'm going to look around the yard first."

Sure enough, as she looked under the bushy camellia, there tangled in the branches, but nearly hidden from sight, was a bag. She called Officer Brumell over to see the sack.

"I didn't want to touch it, but I think this is the sack with the stuff from the Osmund's home."

The officer reached in and pulled the sack out. It was a doubled plastic sack that you might find in any store. He opened it up. Inside were some canned food, some loose change with a few dollar bills. Further digging netted some bottles of pills.

The officer chuckled. "I wonder if the kid knew these pills were for arthritis."

Laryn smiled back. "Dumb kid. We probably did him a favor by catching him. If he was going to sell them as a street drug and when the buyer found out they didn't work the way they thought, the kid would probably have ended up dead."

"You could be right. I'll take this stuff back to the precinct where we'll question the kid. You're back on duty later today, right?"

"Yes, unless you need me to come down right now."

"It won't hurt to let the kid cool his heels for awhile. Finish your run." He did a half way salute mixed with a wave goodbye and left in his patrol car.

Laryn went back to the Osmund's house and knocked on the door.

Mrs. Osmund answered. ""Oh, come on in, girl. I'm so glad you were around to help us. They told me they would bring my husband home after they checked him out. I hope they do. I'm a little shaken and don't think I should be driving right now. Could I fix you a cup of tea. I sure need some." The more she talked the more agitated she became.

"No thank you, but that's why I came back. To see if you're all right and if they don't bring him home, please give me a call and I'll bring him home. I'll be on duty in a couple more hours. I'll give you my cell phone number. Don't give it out, but call me anytime your might need my help."

"You're such a kind girl. Your mother must be very proud of you." Mrs. Osmund was calming down.

Laryn laughed, "Yeah, she is when she's not being a match-maker."

The old lady gave a giggle that belied her age. "We mothers tend to do that, dear. Thank you again for your help."

Laryn nodded. "I'll let you get back to your routine. I'll check in later to see how your husband made out, if I don't see you sooner. Have a good day, ma'am."

Laryn continues her jog. Her normal route was a circle. Since she was on the downside anyway she continued straight away. She felt like she had already done a day's worth of work, but still had time to contemplate life. Her heart was still pumping extra hard from all the excitement, so she slowed her jog down to a trot.

Since it was on her route, Laryn decide to buy a healthy Hougie sandwich for her breakfast and a power drink. She never knew if she'd get another meal while on duty. With this later shift, it didn't work well to eat supper late at night. It was a bummer that she wouldn't be able to hit the Athletic Club and hassle Quinn. Now that they had eaten a dinner at her folk's house, she felt she knew him better and could bounce jokes off him without looking too forward flirting with him.

Part of Laryn's work route included the truck rest stop café. She thought while she was there she would see if the trucker, who might have taken Maya Toreno on a trip, had returned yet or maybe Maya was back at work.

The waitress on duty told her, "No, we've not seen Maya, but the fellow that she was flirting with before she left came by to eat lunch and he's left now."

Laryn thanked her and went on to finish her route for the day. Again, she checked the high school as the kids went home. Again, things were quiet or else she'd better change her schedule. They get wise to the police route times and just have to wait until she leaves to start screwing around in things better left alone.

She checked out a dog on the loose. As the culprit was calmly trotting down the sidewalk, an anxious owner was rushing after him. Laryn stopped and got out of the squad car. Startled, the dog stopped and looked around. Spying it's mistress it took of running towards her. It literally jumped into the woman's arm. She waved at Laryn and mouthed a 'thank you'. Laryn saluted back, then got in the car, wrote the report up with the solution and left. She checked into the station a few times during the day. It was now dark and getting close to the end of her duty. She had to check a business door that might have been left open and that was it. What a boring day after such a hectic start.

On the way to her apartment, she bought some lemon grass soup. She'd have it with a piece of toast; nothing heavy before she went to bed. A week on this schedule and she might think of getting a different job. In her mind, she seemed to be a 'nine to five' person.

At the apartment, she glanced at the answering machine. It had two messages. She put her soup on the table and hit the button.

The first message was from Estelle Baronia. *"Hi Laryn, it's Estelle. My mother said you were wondering if I had called you. I would have had I thought you wanted to hear from me, but it wasn't me who called you. Maybe we could meet for coffee sometime. Take care, girl."*

The second message was from Quinn Madden. *"I enjoyed our dinner together. I know you can't come to the club this week, so how about breakfast at Denny's before you go to work. I need to eat and so do you. Call me"*

Laryn carefully wrote his number down as he gave it to her. She would call him after she ate her soup. She was starving to death and lemon grass soup was one of her favorites.

Laryn made her call to Quinn. She reached the Health Club. Darn, she was hoping it was his private number. The receptionist wondered how she could help her.

"If Quinn Madden is around, may I speak to him?"

"Yes, we're just closing up. I'll call him to the phone."

A lightly breathless Quinn answered. *"This is Quinn."*

"This is Laryn. I'd love to have breakfast with you, but may I suggest a place up on the hill. It's just a small hole-in-the-wall, Mom and Pop restaurant. I love the biscuits and gravy, with a glass of freshly squeezed orange juice and strong coffee."

Quinn laughed, *"I see you already have your order in. Sure, introduce me to a new place to eat and I'll critique the menu to see if it's healthy."*

"Hey! I didn't say to critique it. I like my food and I work hard enough to eat whatever I like."

"Sure you do right now, but one of these days the pounds will appear and you'll wish you had paid more attention to what you ate while you were younger."

Laryn huffed, "You make it sound like you're an old man. Did you always watch what you ate?"

"Pretty much so. Being a weight pusher and competing in the muscleman programs makes you very aware of your food and energy levels. Listen, Laryn, I need to finish closing this place up. I'll meet you in the morning at your hole-in-the-wall place. What time?"

"Is six too early for a man of your advanced age?" smirked Laryn

"Yeah, it is, but anything for you, Laryn." He laughed as he hung up, getting in the last word.

Laryn showered and got ready for bed. Life was on an upswing. She had a breakfast date with Quinn. How much better could life get?

ON AND OFF THE BEAT #4

Laryn dressed for her run wearing knee leggings and a tight sports running top in turquoise and black. Let Quinn see that there was no fat on her body. Just tight muscles and firm boobs. Looking in the mirror, she thought the color enhanced her eyes, or were they always this sparkly? Nah, she shook her head. It was Quinn. Meeting with a good looking man made most women's eyes sparkle.

Looking out her window to the river, while she drank her sports energy drink, calmed her. She couldn't see anything but a dark ribbon cutting through the city. Just knowing the river was there was enough for her.

Her black cat clock rolled its eyes at her as she glanced at it and left for her run. Up the hill towards the hospital, past Forest Park, past some of the schools and Assisted Living places was the little Mom and Pop place she had selected. It was close to half way between her run and Quinn's. If he brought his car, boy, would she crow about it. She grinned at the thought.

She needed to slow down. There was no need for perspiration. This was more for endurance and to keep her body is shape. Some people swam laps or did home exercises, she ran around town.

With the glow of the morning light, she could see another jogger. She presumed it was Quinn. They both were nearing the restaurant.

She stopped outside on the sidewalk and bent over to catch her breath. Straightening up as Quinn approached, she quipped, "Good morning, handsome."

"Why, good morning to you, too, Slick."

She looked surprise, "Why 'slick'?"

"Because you look like one of those Grey Hound dogs they use in racing."

Disgusted, Laryn snorted, "I look like a dog?" She glared at him.

Quinn shrugged his shoulder and splayed his hands, "I guess that came out wrong. Blame it on the early morning and I haven't had my morning coffee yet."

Laryn looked him over. He was still jogging in place cooling down. His hands were spread wide and he was shrugging his shoulders. It made for a funny sight.

She started laughing. "Okay, I'll buy that since you now look like one of those jumping-jacks you see in stores where they pull the bottom string and the clown starts doing jumping-jacks."

He grinned, "Are we even now in exchanging insults this morning? Can we eat soon, I'm ready to expire?"

They went in the door. Quinn put his hand on her back as he ushered her to a table. He could feel Laryn quiver as he did so, but didn't comment on it. He sniffed. The coffee was freshly brewed and smelled wonderful. The place had probably just opened up as he and Laryn exchanged insults outside. A pleasant older lady came to take their order.

"Good morning, Laryn. You must be out for your morning run? Coffee I presume?"

"Yes, Mrs. Dolittle and this morning we're going to eat, too. You can leave a menu, so Quinn, here can critique it. He's a health-food nut from down at the Athletic Club."

Mrs. Dolittle held out her hand. "I'm glad to meet you Mr. Quinn."

Quinn stood up, "Like wise, Mrs. Dolittle, and it's just Quinn, please."

She put the menus on the table. "I'll give you a few minutes to peruse it."

Quinn leaned into Laryn's space. "See, this lady knows what's good for you. There is oatmeal on the menu, fresh fruit dish, no cholesterol eggs, and turkey sausage. I'll bet you've been eating healthy and just didn't know it."

"Oh no! Not healthy! I thought I'd gotten away from that when I left home. Mom just told me to stop by Mrs. Dolittle's if I got hungry. I don't do healthy." Laryn knew the menu was healthy, but it wouldn't hurt to string Quinn along. If the food was good, she didn't mind healthy, but to eat some of the granolas with the blue milk just didn't do it for her.

"You're a fraud, Laryn Scott. You knew this place would meet with my approval."

Mrs. Dolittle came and took their order.

Laryn ordered her biscuits and gravy, fresh squeezed orange juice and coffee. Quinn nodded and ordered the oatmeal, fruit bowl and coffee. Mrs Dolittle left to put the order in to her husband, the cook.

"So, do you know everyone on town, or just the ones on your route?" Quinn steeples his hands together under his chin, elbows on the table.

Laryn shook her head. "Not everyone, but a big percentage. I went to school with some, played sports with others, joined the Y.M.C.A. and even picked strawberries in the fields. I'm good at names, faces and now I'm working on voices."

Interested now, Quinn leaned forward, with just one arm on the table. "And why the voices?"

Laryn looked puzzled, "Didn't I tell you about the case I'm working on when we were at Mom's last week?"

"If you did I must have been too interested in your whole family and the delicious meal."

Laryn shook her head. "How like a man to think of his stomach when I was telling such and interesting story."

"Tell me again. I'm listening with bated breath this time. I'm all ears and I won't take my eyes off of you." To himself he thought, yeah, I can't take my eyes off you. Your eyes are like blue skies.

Laryn blinked at the intensity of his attention. "Well, the other day as I entered my apartment, the answering machine was blinking. When I pushed the button for play-back, this person called me 'Laryn' and said he was going to kill her, then there was a scuffle and the phone was hung up. I'm going through my memory of voices to see if I can find out who called me."

Quinn shook his head, "You say she didn't give her name and thought she was going to be killed?"

"Right. It was the quiet hang-up that convinced me of the truth of the message."

Mrs. Dolittle brought their meal to the table. "Is there anything else I can do for you?" They shook their heads. Mrs. Dolittle left them to their meal. They ate in silence.

Quinn rubbed his stomach. "That was good oatmeal. It had a nutty flavor, so I know it was homemade from scratch."

Laryn quietly laughed, "And my biscuits and gravy were good, too."

They paid for their meal and left. Quinn ran with Laryn down the hill until he needed to branch off towards the Health Club, then with a salute he pealed off.

It was dark when Laryn got the call to check out a cougar sighting. It was up on the hill surrounded by treed areas. There very well could be a cougar up there. She asked the dispatcher, "Did you call the Fish and Wildlife service?"

"Yes we did, but you were in the vicinity and could respond before they can get there."

Laryn took off up the hill. She didn't use the siren or the emergency lights. This wasn't an emergency and would just frightened people. She arrived at the address. The porch light was on and people were looking out the window, obviously waiting for someone to come. Laryn checked her weapon before she opened the door of the cruiser. She put it back in her holster, but didn't buckle it down. She could draw it like an old-time cowboy. When she got to the porch, the door opened and a gentleman came out.

"It's in the back yard. We were barbecuing and left our mess out on the table. We went inside to eat our ice cream since it was getting cold outside and then put the kids to bed. When my wife and I went out to clean the table off, there was this green-eyed, bean-eating animal hunched down on the table and it hissed at us like a cougar. It was too dark to see anymore than that. We ran back inside and locked the door and called 911."

Just then a Fish and Wildlife van pulled up. The fellow got out holding a rifle. A little over-kill thought Laryn, but all she knew about killing animals was that she didn't approve of it unless it was necessary.

She greeted the officer. "I'm Laryn Scott."

He shook her hand, "I'm Dave Dunlap. What's the score?"

Laryn updated him. "Backyard barbecue. When they came out to clean the table, there were green eyes staring at them and it was hissing."

Dave nodded, "Follow me," pointing his gun towards the sidewalk that lead to the backyard.

Laryn didn't move. "I need you to know, I don't approve of killing an animal unless it really needs it."

Still all business, he nodded to her, "It's a tranquilizer gun."

She grinned in the dim light. "Lead on McDuff," referring to a dog that was a detective in a cartoon. She wondered if he knew the show.

He shook his head at her thinking she was such a flake. She drew her heavy duty flashlight and pointed it over his shoulder as they proceeded around the house. Laryn's heart pounded as they came to the backyard she didn't know if it was from fear or just the excitement of the chase. She followed the light with the way he was pointing the rifle. At first they saw nothing, but then a pan fell to the ground. Laryn's heart stopped and she could feel Dave flinch. They both flashed to the table. There were the green eyes starring back at them and it was pawing the air and hissing. It was truly mad about being interrupted during its meal. It bared its teeth and hissed even louder when the intruders didn't leave. Dave had his gun pointed at it.

A little more flashing the light around showed it wasn't a tawny brown, but a black-eyed bandit. There standing on its hind-legs, hissing and pawing the air, was a mad raccoon. The bean-eating cougar was a hissing and snarling raccoon. Not that a raccoon can't be dangerous with the threat of rabies, but after you were expecting a cougar to pounce on you, a raccoon was a let-down. Laryn shook her head.

Dave stoically looked back at Laryn. "I don't think I'll need the rifle tonight. I'll set a trap tomorrow and I'll probably get him then. The raccoon knows where the food is now, so he will come back."

They left the fellow to finish his meal and went around to the front porch to inform the homeowner about the raccoon.

The man and his wife laughed at their mistake. "But he hissed like a cougar," was his face-saving retort.

It was past Dave's time on duty. He was tired and hungry. "You don't happen to be about to go off duty are you? I'm starving and hate to eat alone. I'll even buy you a cup of coffee if you're not off duty yet."

Laryn took a good look at the fellow. He was close in age and a bit stiff, but he was a man and he was willing to buy her a cup of coffee.

"I'm close enough to being off my shift. Let me take the cruiser back to the station and get my car. Denny's is open all night. I'll meet you there without the rifle and badge, I hope?"

He frowned at her. "Of course. I don't flaunt my rifle at just any old thing. It has to be bigger than a bean-eating raccoon."

Laryn grinned, "I'm so glad to hear that. She saluted as she climbed in her cruiser to leave.

Laryn was at Denny's within twenty minutes. She saw Dave waiting for her in his Fish and Wildlife van. She met him at the door. Inside they were led to a corner table. Even though Laryn would be going home to sleep, she ordered coffee and so did Dave.

Laryn perused the menu. "Since I'm off duty now, I'm going to eat. On this shift, I eat a huge breakfast at about noon, but then it's just snacks the rest of the day and a bowl of soup at night. By about the end of this week-long swing shift duty, I'm hungry for a good supper."

"Since I don't change my shift that often, I usually eat right on time, unless I'm called out. like now. However, I have no problems sleeping even in the back of the van." Dave chose something from the menu and put it to the side the table.

Seeing they were both ready to order, the waitress came, wrote down what they wanted and left taking the menus with her.

"So, Laryn Scott, are you married, going with someone or a lesbo?"

"No I'm not." Raising her eyebrows, she retorted. "So Dave Dunlap, are you married, going with someone or gay?"

Dave smiled at her comeback. She had true grit. "What would you do if I said I was gay?"

Laryn grinned back at him. "Not a darned thing. The few I know of are very nice people and make good friends to most women."

"Good answer, but I'd eat our dinner and wave goodbye never to be seen again. It isn't that I have anything against the gay community, but I don't have that much in common with them to even be friends. I hunt and fish and I doubt they would kill anything even to eat it."

Laryn looked at him. "I don't fish and hunt either, but I'm into all kinds of sports. My brother and I were on every team made and did very well. He watched all my games and I rooted for him in all of his. He's part of the coaching staff up at the high school."

"Yeah, I played sports in high school, but that was the end of my organized sports days. I love to hike in the mountains, take pictures of the wildlife and anything else that strikes my fancy."

"I like to hike, but I'm not into taking the pictures. The groups I hike with are too noisy to see any wildlife. Your hikes sound better than mine."

He looked interested. 'Say, the next time you have a day off, I could take you out on a hike. We might see a wild animal or two."

Laryn thought a minute. Nothing came up in her memory that had her booked for her next day off. "Sure, I'd like that."

He gave her his card. "Call me when you know and I'll arrange my work schedule to fit your day off. Do you have hiking boots?"

"Yes, I have boots that would work. I had them on when we went to see the bean-eating cougar. If I have to beat the brush, I wanted to be ready. Actually, most of the time I wear those boots. You never know when you might have to take off after someone and that might entail going over the hills and through the dales to grandmother's house we go." She stopped her sing-song voice and added. "They aren't heavy duty, but they are comfortable."

"I suppose they are the 'spit and polish' type?"

"Of course. I can't go around looking like a bum, unless I'm undercover and so far I've not done that duty." She grinned again. "I'm too easy to spot."

Dave looked surprised. He then looked her over. "I suppose you are. You're too pretty to live in a dumpster." Funny, he hadn't paid that much attention to her until she said she was easy to spot. At this point, he felt he had just found someone to go on a hike with. Darn it, now he would think about her and thinking about a woman brought into the mix an attraction he hadn't thought of before.

They got up to pay the bill and leave. Outside they parted with Dave saying, "Call me!"

Laryn nodded.

When she got to her apartment, the telephone answering machine was blinking. Even though it was late at night, she felt she needed to know what the message was all about. She reluctantly hit the replay button.

"*Miz Scott, this is Feliz Toreno. I'm getting worried about my Maya. She no come home or call me in a month now. Her work keeps calling to ask when she will come in again. I no know what to tell them. Call me if you think this is something I should worry about.*" He left his number as if Laryn didn't know it by heart.

This was terrible news to her. She had hoped her call about someone being killed was just a hoax. Now she'd worry the bone all night. It was too late to do anything about it right now, but come morning, she'd work on the problem before she had to go to work.

ON AND OFF THE BEAT #5

The next morning, Laryn didn't want to get up, but her body just couldn't sleep past six o'clock. If she was awake, she might as well get up and do her run. It was raining so she dressed in her racing attire with her hair under a baseball cap. She shook her head at her image. It reminded her of Quinn calling her 'Slick' because the clothes contoured to her body.

Now if she could only wear blinders like they did for horses, she might not see any illegal activities and could do the run in short order. She needed to think about Mr. Toreno's problem. Running was good for that. It cleared her head.

Her run was a good one, but no immediate solution to Mr. Toreno's problem came to mind. It still boiled down to the trucker who might have been the last one to see Maya before she disappeared. That meant back to the Truck Stop to see if she could get a line on who that was. Her other option was to look at the telephone records of Mr. Toreno's and see to whom Maya might have called prior to her disappearance. A reverse directory was good for that.

She got out of her wet clothes and took a nice hot shower. She dressed in her jeans and a sweatshirt with a Mount Vernon school logo on it. She didn't want to look like a cop when she went to the Truck Stop. She could question the waitresses again, but wouldn't scare off any potential suspect if he was there and the big question was 'if'.

Laryn needed breakfast anyway and the Truck Stop had a hardy one. Maybe not up to Quinn's standards, but all she needed was something to keep her full until she got off duty tonight. Just a few more days of this lousy schedule and she would progress back to her regular one. She would dance with joy.

A different waitress waited on her.

"My name is Lucy and I'll be your waitress this morning. Could I get you something to drink? Juice? Coffee?"

"You're a new waitress? I'm usually waited on by Maya." Laryn didn't like to lie, but sometimes the questioning took a turn you just had to follow.

"Maya hasn't come in for a month, so they hired me. I really needed the job, so I hope I can serve you as well as she did."

Laryn nodded to her and smiled. "I'm sure you will do just fine. I'll start with a cup of coffee and orange juice with the *trucker's special* breakfast."

"Good choice. I'll bring your coffee right away." And she left to get the coffee pot which she used to top off other cups as she made her way back to Laryn's table.

Laryn thought she'd push a little. As the waitress filled her cup and made to go back to her station, Laryn casually asked, "Maya used to complain about the truckers hitting on her. Do you find that a problem?"

A grin issued forth. "Oh, they don't mean any harm. It just seems to be their way to start a conversation. I roll with the punches and smile a lot and the tips are better that way."

Laryn softly laughed. "I'll just bet they are."

The waitress nodded, "Your breakfast is up. I'll bring it right over."

So much for her questioning, thought Laryn. At least her breakfast would make this all worth while.

Back at her apartment, she put in a call to Feliz Toreno. She got the answering machine. "Mr. Toreno, this is Laryn Scott. I'm on the swing shift and since you are just barely out of my jurisdiction, could you set up a time I could meet with you from six o'clock in the morning until noon. I would like to see who delivered your alfalfa and your phone records to see who Maya might have called." Laryn left a number for her home phone. With the answering machine she could check back without having to use her memory which was sluggish on this shift.

She did a thorough cleaning of her apartment. This was the only good thing she could say about swing shift. She could do things during the day that normally she couldn't do on her regular shift without using up her evenings. She made a batch of chocolate chip cookies, but only cooked one sheet full. She froze the rest for later use. It was time to go to work.

She took a plate of cookies to the break-room at work. Today she found out she would be riding with Bay Renaldo. Bay's real name was Baynard, but no one called him that on fear for their life. Bay was a huge man with plenty of buff, but no muscles that Laryn would drool over. He was serious about his work, so there would be no jokes or wisecracks today. Laryn knew that the police work wasn't funny, but Bay wouldn't appreciate the story of the *bean eating cougar that turned out to be a raccoon.* She thought it was at least light-weight humor. She'd have laughed at the ploy.

Bay greeted her like a bulldog who could talk. "We're going to be on the lookout for gangs on the prowl and drug deals. I'll drive and you keep a sharp lookout."

Laryn nodded her head and thought to herself, *"Yes, my lord and master."*

Bay nodded back in acknowledgement. He barely remembered that she was a female. He knew she was a fast runner and could shoot straight. That's all he needed in a partner, oh, and don't talk unless spoken to.

They cruised around in complete silence.

After about two long, long hours, Laryn spotted a group of men in the park.

She commented, "Men up ahead."

Bay grunted.

Laryn supposed that meant he saw what she saw. As they approached, the men dispersed in different directions. Either their meeting was done or they didn't want to speak to the cops. Laryn figured they would never catch anybody this way, but at least it stopped whatever might be going on. It was groups like this that sometimes ended up in a shootout because someone got pissed off about some small thing.

Just then a car burned rubber ahead of them as shots rang out. Bay nearly snapped Laryn's neck as he took off after the perpetrator. As they sped by the incident, Laryn saw someone down, but that person waved them on pointing towards the speeding car. She called 911 and told them to send an ambulance to the address she called out. She then called the police dispatcher and told them about the high speed chase they were on and called for backup, plus one for the downed person.

Her seatbelt was nearly cutting off her neck as Bay squealed around corners. Her heart was pounding as they chased the perps over the Skagit River Bridge and through West Mount Vernon. Out on the flats they really hit the gas. Nearing a sharp corner Bay eased off, but the car ahead kept going, careening out of control and into a vacant field. Soon it bogged down in a muddy area, but Laryn was already out and running towards the car.

She watched carefully as she ran. If anyone got out of the car, she'd zigzag running since she knew they'd had a gun of some kind. She could hear the thunk, squish, thunk, squish, thunk, squish of the giant Bay running behind her.

The car was gunning its motor and spewing mud up behind it. She was almost there when the door opened and someone tried to get out. She hit the door as she sped by, causing an earsplitting scream. She turned in front of the car and was at the other door, just as Bay came up to the one she had slammed but had bounced back off the arm of the perp. With her gun out and pointed at those in the car, she saw they all had their hands raised, but were looking at Bay.

She could hear police sirens in the background and the smell of moist dirt came up to confront her. Bay had picked up the gun the driver had had in his hand when he was trying to climb out. She kept her gun on the occupants as Bay drew each one out and cuffed them. The driver was writhing in pain on the muddy ground. One turned out to be a female. Bay gruffly asked Laryn to come around and frisk her. He really did sound like a bulldog that could talk. Laryn wanted to laugh but knew it was the adrenaline rush that had her over re-acting.

Other police cars stopped on the road and helped load the suspects into several cars. One was going to take the driver up to emergency to check his arm. The rest would cool their heels in jail until statements could be taken.

And so ended another day in the life of a police officer, thought Laryn. Bulldog, otherwise known as Bay, told her she did a good job and turned away to handle some of the paperwork.

She heard the person who had been shot was just a person out walking his dog. The car full of perpetrators had wanted his money and when his dog went after them, growling and barking, they let out a burst of gunfire, missing the dog and hitting him in the leg. He'd live, but the officer that went to the scene of the crime said the victum was still screaming about getting retaliation for just walking his dog in a supposedly quiet neighborhood. "Get the perps and I'll gladly testify," was his angry comment.

After giving her statement, Laryn went home and was almost too tired to eat. At home her answering machine had left her two messages. *"Laryn, it's your mother. Please come to Sunday dinner. Your shift should be over and we've missed you. Pot roast with all the trimmings, see ya."* Second message: *"Miz. Scott. This is Feliz. I have coffee at siete, I mean seven. Please you join me then. I have bizcocho hot from the oven and miel."*

Laryn got out her high school Spanish book. Okay, biscuits and honey or molasses. Ah! Good. Something to look forward to. She'd have to drive out there and skip her run. She had a bowl of cold cereal, brushed her teeth, showered and went to bed.

The next morning was raining and dreary, just the kind of day to go out and interview an anxious father about his missing daughter. Bummer! She arrived at Mr. Toreno's at exactly seven o'clock in the morning. He opened the door to Laryn with the smell of coffee and biscuits waffling out the door before him.

———

He gestured, "Please come in, Miz Scott."

"Thank you, Mr. Toreno. Something smells good in here."

"Si, tis my biscuits. Even my mouth waters at the smell."

He led Laryn out to his family kitchen. It was the farm type where all persons could gather and sit around the table to gossip or plan the day. He had coffee cups and small plates set for them.

"Please sit down and I'll serve the biscuits and coffee. You take leche, I mean milk?"

"No, just black."

Mr. Toreno served the biscuits and honey. Laryn took one and split it and added the honey. It was like eating two crusts and was delicious. She closed her eyes in appreciation.

"It's so good. Thank you, Mr. Toreno."

He beamed. "You are too kind."

Laryn took a sip of the hot coffee, "Tell me, Mr. Toreno, when did you last see Maya or talked to her?"

"I see her the night before she is to leave on her vacation. That is the last time I talked to her, also."

"Was she happy to be going on this vacation?"

"Si. She very happy. She tell me she will be safe with this fellow. He will bring her home on his trip back from California. He will get another load of something to bring back up here. She say she will be gone only a week or two. Now, she gone a month. I worry." He looked downcast.

Laryn reached over and cradled his hand in comfort. "Do you know the fellow's name or who he works for?"

"Not really. She calls him Bubba. He owns his own truck, so she thinks he's rich. I know he's just a trucker and not rich. She not thinks straight when she thinks she's in love."

Laryn nodded her head in commiseration with the father of her friend. Her memory of Maya was that she was a little boy-crazy, but all high school girls were boy-crazy, even she drooled at any muscle that walked by.

Changing the subject, she asked, "Who delivered your alfalfa?"

Mr. Toreno got up to get his paperwork. "I copy all the papers you asked for. I went to late-night store and copy machine."

He brought the papers over to the table. Sorting through them, he picked out a sales receipt. It listed the company Mr. Toreno had ordered from and how many tons. It wasn't a large order, but enough to demand a large truck, thought Laryn. The signature of the delivery man was certainly indistinct just a Mr. Toreno had said. There was a telephone number of the place he had purchased the load from. She would check that out later.

"Okay, now about the telephone bills. Did she have a cell phone?"

"Si. She had one but she must have taken it with her. I no see it around."

"Are these the bills here, both your home phone and her cell phone?"

"Si. I copy them for you. I need originals for my farm."

Laryn shuffled the bills together. "Where do you work, Mr. Toreno?"

"I work in warehouse of one of the growers here in the valley." He named the familiar grower.

Laryn finished off her coffee and biscuit and made to get up. "Thank you for all your help. I'll take this back to my place and call a few numbers. I hope we can get a lead on Maya's where-abouts."

Mr. Toreno nodded his head. 'You will tell me if you get any information. I'm really worried, now. Maya is a good girl and always has kept me informed where she at and where she going. She take care of me when her momma died. I miss her."

Laryn shook the man's hand. "I'll try, Mr. Toreno, I'll really try." Laryn thought a minute. "I think you should report Maya as missing to the County Sheriff's department. After a month of her being gone, they should listen and not brush Maya off as a run-away."

He nodded his head again.

On her way to her apartment, she thought of all she had learned. It wasn't much to go on and the heartbreak would be if Maya never came home. The old man had no one but his daughter.

ON AND OFF THE BEAT #6

At her apartment, Laryn had time to make a few phone calls. She called the place that Mr. Toreno had ordered his alfalfa from. It was a farm that sold to warehouses. They didn't know who had delivered the alfalfa. The warehouse arranged the deliveries. That they had been paid was all they cared about. They gave her the name of the warehouse they sold to.

Laryn didn't have time to follow that lead. She called her mother instead. "Hi, Mom. I'll be coming to dinner on Sunday."

"I'm so glad, Laryn. Dayne is bringing Quinn again. Quinn is giving a talk to Dayne's team. Since it is Sunday, the team is meeting late in the day. I won't be serving at 2:00 o'clock like I usually do. It will be more like 5:00 and casual dress as the boys are coming from the gym. I hope your father doesn't perish from hunger."

Laryn laughed, "I'm sure he'll survive. I have to leave for work. Bye for now. See you on Sunday."

She glanced at her clock. The cat rolled its eyes at her as if it knew her heart was racing at the news that she would see that hunk of muscles again. "Stop that, black cat! Just mind your minutes and hours and leave my thoughts alone."

She rushed off to dress. She glanced back at the room she was leaving. The cat was still watching her rolling its eyes, her juice glass with the face of a girl with riotous red hair was watching her and the hunk-of-the-month on the front of her magazine left on the coffee table was looking quizzically at her. Did a guilty conscience rate all those eyes following her?

At work, she was in charge of a group of teenagers that had been busted for drinking and probably using drugs. Even though she stood guard, the real reason for the surveillance was to see that none of them died off while waiting for their arraignment. They would either go to Juvenile Hall for the

44

night or their parents would pick them up, or if one pasted out, he or she might end up in the hospital for the night.

This was not a fun job. They harassed her, mocking her height and buzz-cut hair. They were loud and obnoxious. In a group, they were tough. When taken individually into a room for interrogation, they were timid, just a kid caught doing something he shouldn't be doing.

She stood her ground and helped with the pat-down of the girls. Even the girls were mouthy. One asked if she was enjoying copping a feel. Laryn hoped that one had to stay the night in Juvie. In her mind, she kept chanting *'we're saving their lives, we're saving their lives.'*

She had heard the kids were standing on the river bank, with a bonfire blazing, daring each other to swim the river, the death defying Skagit River. When they were busted, a couple ran for the water, but the cold had them standing hip-deep in freezing water and paralyzed because of it.

Just then one smart-mouthed girl rolled her eyes and started to fall. Laryn caught her and quickly lowered her to the floor. She yelled out, "Girl down, call the paramedics."

Laryn checked her vitals. Her pulse was out-of-sight, her breathing was shallow, but at least she was breathing. She started to convulse, shaking and squirming around. All Laryn could do was make sure she didn't hurt herself hitting anything. Some of the other girls started to cry. "Is she dying?"

Laryn looked at them, "I don't think so, but this is what might happen when you drink or experiment with drugs. It's a life and death decision you have to make."

Just then the paramedics came to pick up the girl. She had peed all over the floor. Laryn thought, *shoot, now I have to clean up that mess.* She was looking around for something to mop it up with, when a trustee came with a bucket and mop.

The other girls were mumbling, "Oh, gross!"

Laryn put her hands together, "Oh, thank you, thank you, kind sir."

The trustee grinned back at her. "All in a days job here, ma'am."

Laryn breathed a sigh of relief. Her shift was over. None of the kids had died. The girl taken to the hospital was a diabetic and should have known better than to drink alcohol. She had tomorrow off before she started her day shift.

Going into her apartment, her 'secretary' was beeping to her. What would she do without her answering machine? It reported trouble, but it also kept her informed of what was going on in her life.

She punched the replay button. *"Laryn. This is Dave Dunlap. I'm still waiting for your call to go on a wildlife hike. Call me anytime."* Laryn wrote his number down, even though she had it someplace. It was late, but she poured herself a glass of wine to unwind. She had a funky glass that could make her smile. It was a painted pottery glass she had found at a garage sale. A bright-eyed face was painted on it. Dangly earrings hung down from make-shift ears with a matching necklace which squirreled around the stem that made up the long neck of the kissy-lipped girl

Laryn sat down with her drink at her table. "I had a really bad day. There were these kids that we busted and probably saved some of their lives. I guess we did good." Laryn wiggled her glass back and forth. The earrings swung a 'yes' vote.

Laryn took a swallow. "Should I call Dave back and arrange a hike to see wildlife?" The glass hesitated for a second and then slowly nodded again. Laryn smiled. "It's so good of you to be so agreeable."

She took her last sip. Jeeze, she was talking to an empty headed wine glass. If she stayed on this schedule much longer, they would have to lock her up in a straight jacket. Yes, she would call Dave tomorrow. She needed a rational, stoic person to bring her back to earth.

The next morning, she had slept in beyond her six o'clock schedule. She felt she must have been really tired to do that or was it that glass of wine? Laryn made her call to Dave. It must have been his cell phone as he professionally answered on the second ring. *"Dunlap speaking."*

"Hello, Mr. Dunlap. This is Laryn Scott and I'm returning your call."

Such a change in voice quality. *"Wow, Laryn. So you are returning my call, and so, when can you go on this wildlife hike I have planned for you?"*

Laryn felt like giggling. He seemed to be thrilled she had called. "How about tomorrow? I know it's Sunday, but I do have the day off and my mother has planned a late dinner. I don't have to be there until five o'clock and it's casual dress. If you like pot roast with all the trimmings, I could even ask you to dinner."

He was taken aback. Her mother didn't know him. He could be a serial killer. It didn't set well to be invited to a Sunday dinner when you didn't know the family and they didn't know you. *"I don't know—? They don't know me."*

"Aw, come on. My brother invites strangers all the time. He's bringing his friend, Quinn, after football practice."

"Look, Laryn. I'll pick you up at ten o'clock and we'll go from there. If we're still speaking to each other after a day of viewing the wildlife, we'll call your family and ask if there is time and enough food to put another plate on the table."

"Fair enough, Dave. I'll have my boots on and comfortable walking clothes. Do I bring a packed lunch?"

"No, I'll take care of all of that. I always carry a small backpack. It has the ten essentials for survival, plus my water bottle, fresh fruit, candy bars and a sandwich that doesn't take ice to keep it fresh."

"Wow! All of that and do you get long ears and bray by evening?"

There was silence on the other end. Darn! Her wild mouth probably did in this adventure.

"Oh, I get it. You think I'm a pack mule. It would take more that fifty pounds of packing to get me to take a mule into the back country. Forty pounds usually is my limit and my daypack probably weighs ten pounds at the max. I think we'll survive without the braying mule."

"I'm sorry, Dave, for being such a jackass. Darn, now I can't get the long-eared, four-legged critter off my mind. Anyway, you'll love my brother and Quinn. They horse around all the time. Darn, again. Okay, my mother is a good cook that should do it and it won't be a horse meat roast."

"Sorry, Laryn, I've got another call coming in and I've got to take it. I'll pick you up at your place. See you tomorrow."

Her voice was sad, "Bye for now, Dave."

Dave picked her up right on time. She figured he would be punctual. He had a different SUV than the one he drove around for work. Even though it was washed, it was a dirty green color. Laryn felt he probably didn't want to be spotted if he wanted to park and look over an area. She knew this is what she would drive if she was a game warden.

He wore a khaki shirt and cargo pants. He had a camouflage hat on. Laryn looked him over. He could have blended into the forest just by stepping out of his vehicle. Shock! Shock! His clothes made his eyes green. She didn't know if she'd ever seen green eyes before. They looked nice and he was a nice man. Now, they'd see if they could get along for a whole day.

Dave motioned Laryn to get in. She'd been waiting at the curb for him. Those long legs just stepped right into the cab without the usual hopping around even some of his partners had to do.

Her pink baseball hat had a curly-cue ribbon and said, 'For the cure.' He wondered if she did the *'Run for the Cure'* marathon for cancer. He appreciated her skin-tight pants that seem to stretch when she stepped into the vehicle. Her pink and black plaid shirt had a tank top underneath and her light-weight jacket was tied casually around her neckline. She obviously knew how to layer-dress for the day. She was a fine looking woman. He'd kind of thought that in the dim light of the porch at the 'bean-eating raccoon' home.

"I thought I'd take you to the viewing station by Concrete. The elk have been congregating there lately. Sometimes they swim the river to graze on some people's yards on the South Skagit. Let's hope today they are on this side."

They proceeded up SR 20 to the viewing station. It was just outside the small town of Concrete. Dave spoke very little, leaving her to muse over the outing. Laryn wondered how the local winery could save their vines from destruction by a whole herd of elk. She knew the farmers thought they were the bane of their lives. Also, the lawns of homes would take a beating when an elk herd walked through it leaving deep holes to mow over.

However, when they parked facing the huge field full of the magnificent creatures, Laryn felt awed by them. "Look at the horns on that big bull."

Dave dug around under his seat and pulled out binoculars. "Here, look at him through these."

Laryn took the glasses and adjusted them to her sight. "Wow! He turned around and is looking at us. I think he'd charge us if we got out of the rig."

Dave grinned at her. "Nah, he's just postulating for the benefit of his ladies. If we got out of the rig, he'd be more likely to herd them up and move them out. If we made him mad or threatened him, he might turn and fight." He looked over at her. "Just remember that all wild animals are just that; wild. Treat them with respect and try not to aggravate them and quietly back off if possible."

Laryn grinned back. "Like we did for the bean-eating raccoon?"

Dave nodded, "He could have torn us to pieces if we'd have taken his beans away. By-the-way, I caught him the next night in the live trap I'd set. Took him out to a beaver pond area where I released him. He'll be eating fish now."

SR 20 was busy with hay and alfalfa trucks going by Laryn noted. "Is there always this much trafficking of hay and alfalfa on this highway?"

Dave nodded again. "At this time of the year, and until the pass closes, a lot of trucks use this highway. It's closest to the Okanogan hay and grain fields."

He started the vehicle. "Shall we proceed with our wildlife tour?"

"What are we going to see next?"

"I'm never sure we'll see anything, but we're headed up the Baker Lake Highway to maybe see some wild goats."

It had been a wonderful tour. Laryn invited Dave to Sunday dinner at her folk's house. Dave decided to go when Laryn raved about her mother's cooking. He was hungry and so far, the company had been great. Surely her folks must be as nice as she was.

Laryn knocked on the door, but went on in before it was answered. "Hi everybody, I'm home and brought a guest."

Laryn's mother came in from the kitchen. "Hi, sweetie. Who's our guest this time?"

"Mom, I'd like you to meet Dave Dunlap. He took me on a tour to view animals in the wild." She turned to Dave. "I'd like you to meet my mother, Samantha Scott."

"I'm glad to meet you, Mrs. Scott."

Samantha turned to Laryn, "The boys are all in the backyard hanging out. Take your guest out and introduce him around. I'll have dinner on the table in just a few minutes now that you're home."

"Can I help, Mom?"

"No, I just need to set another place and you need to introduce your friend. Go now, dear."

Laryn took Dave through the house and out the kitchen back door. Dave's nose nearly did a one-eighty at the delightful smell coming from the stove. Outside a rousing game of basketball was underway. Laryn's dad sat in a lounge chair reading the Sunday paper. The game stopped when they spotted Laryn with a stranger.

Laryn did the introductions, pointing as she went, "My dad, Jordan, my brother, Dayne and our friend, Quinn, this is Dave."

Dayne came over and put his arm around the pair. "You and Dave can play against Quinn and me."

Laryn looked at Dave, "Do you play?"

Dave shucked his jacket. "Lead on."

It was soon apparent that Laryn was close to pro status. When she was half bent over and her left arm out, it made it almost impossible for anyone to steal the ball. Her butt was lethal, too. Too close and she could upend you by swinging it at you. Dave didn't want to hurt her until he ended up in the grass a few times, then the war was on for both teams. She could score by stiff-arming you and swinging the basketball sideways over her head.

It was apparent to both Dave and Quinn that the brother and sister team were a menace to them, so they stood back and let them fight it out. The ball was finally out of bounds when it went into the neighbor's yard.

"Your fault," yelled Dayne

"Was not, you Neanderthal," retaliated Laryn

Samantha came to the door and called them in to eat. "Wash up." she ordered.

The dinner was delicious. The talk was entertaining and the bantering exciting to the participants. Laryn and Dave told them about viewing the elk, then finding mountain goats on their hike.

"We even saw some baby goats. They were so cute. Then coming back down the trail to get to the SUV a deer ran out in front of us." Laryn was so excited talking about the event her hands were waving around nearly spilling her water. He mother removed Laryn's glass from the path of destruction of good Waterford crystal.

Her children took for granted the Waterford crystal, Spode dinnerware and sterling silver. They had no idea of the value of her Sunday best and probably wouldn't care if they did. To them the food was the value of a Sunday dinner.

Quinn sat there listening to the family talk and thinking he was missing a lot in his life without a family around. Watching Laryn interact with her new fellow made him wish he had been more aggressive in pursuing her. Not that he had given any thought to the wooing of Laryn, but his gut was in a knot as he watched her talk. Did his gut know something he didn't? Was his life at the cross-roads of settling down to a home and family? Was Laryn even interested in a home and family?

He'd spent his whole life in pursuit of his trophies and his healthy life style. Was he up to hamburgers and a beer while watching a sports game on TV? Watching this family interact, hell yes he was! Watching and taking notes on how to become a family member would be his motto for now.

ON AND OFF THE BEAT #7

Laryn's couple of days off were a godsend to her. She still got up and did her run, but took a nap in the afternoon. She shook her head at the thought she was getting old and needed an afternoon nap. Next, she'd be nodding off in church or during commercials on TV.

She changed the water in her fish bowl. It had been her mother's joke. She had no pets, flowers or yard. The bowl had a few fish imbedded in the glass. They really did look like goldfish swimming in the bowl. When she had water in there, a few of her girl friends even looked into the bowl for the fish.

Her girlfriends? She hadn't even had time to talk to any of them. Maybe she'd give one of them a call and see if they wanted to go to a movie or something. There weren't that many of them anymore. They were dropping like flies in winter to the marriage theme and then their husband and family became their world. She supposed that was as it should be. She wondered it she would ever feel like getting married and becoming a housewife. At this moment, she didn't think she was good marriage material. If she ever did think of marriage, she would need to put in for desk duty.

The view of the river called to her. Looking out on the calming slow moving water, she imagined herself pregnant, running after a perpetrator, jumping over a fence and her stomach hitting her in the face as it bounced around. She laughed. Nah! Right now marriage wasn't for her.

The phone rang. When she answered, it was her mother. "Hi, Mom, what can I do for you?"

"Why nothing, dear. I wondered how things were going with the two fine men that have been invited to our Sunday dinners."

Laryn squinted her eyes at the call, "You're not trying to match-make, are you?"

51

"No, dear. I'm not the one who invited the young fellows to dinner, you and Dayne did that."

"Yeah, but that was because of circumstances for both Dayne and me. The fellows needed to eat and it was only polite to invite them to dinner and I know you cook enough to feed an army that your food is excellent and to be proud of." Laryn felt a little boot polishing might work right now.

"And, and what? You don't like the boys?"

"It's not a question of *liking*, it's what you're inferring. If I brought home some girlfriends, would you question Dayne about them?"

"I might if he looked at them the way you looked at those fellows at our table on Sunday."

"Moooom," she wailed. "I was only interested in what they were saying. They were talking wildlife and sports. You and I were just sitting there like bumps on a log. I'd have listened to you if you had been talking quilting." Laryn blushed. Yeah, sure she would. Quilting was about as foreign to her as the wildlife and Dave's day. Now, a good shooting match she could relate to, but she had already been shot down the other Sunday when she had offered shooting lesson to the football team.

"Mom, I've got a call coming in on the other line. I'll have to take it as it might pertain to work."

"Take care, dear. Goodbye."

So she didn't have another line. Maybe her mother wouldn't remember. Now she felt she couldn't even have a date with these fellows or her mother would go all *Wedding Planner* on her.

Laryn went back to her window overlooking the Skagit River, grinning. She wouldn't mind a piece of her mother's cake, be it wedding cake or otherwise. Her mother's cakes were to die for.

The next day, Laryn was back at her desk when they got a call-out on a suspicious smell coming from a house. The lady living there hadn't been seen for about a week. The neighbor, who had called it in, said she had been checking on her neighbor, but hadn't seen anything wrong and a call to the house hadn't had anyone answer it either.

Of course, she got Baynard Renaldo as her partner. Why couldn't it have been friendly Farley Brunell. Bay would drive. God help her if she drove and Bay had to ride with her. Macho man couldn't live with that, she thought. She got her Sam Browne belt that was hanging on a hook in the locker. Laryn's gun was on the upper shelf. She checked that it was loaded. She took her jacket but didn't put it on. Her badge was already on her shirt. Thank God her hair was short so her hat went on without fussing with it.

Some women had to roll their long hair up and stuff it inside their hat. Bay wouldn't have had the patience to wait on that kind of policewoman.

Again, they drove without flashing lights. This wasn't an emergency yet anyway. YET, meant if Bay didn't see something more interesting to take care of than the smelly house they were going to. She knew this guy. *Sit still, don't talk and keep your eyes peeled for trouble.* Maaan, didn't this guy know they were just going to a smelly house. That was enough to write up for today.

They arrived at the address given to them. An elderly lady came out of the house next door as they drove up. She had a breathless voice. "I'm the one who called you. Mrs. Yanek didn't tell me she was going any place and I've not heard from, nor seen her, for about a week. I hope nothing is wrong." The lady pulled her shawl around her shoulders, clearly agitated.

With his jowls bouncing about, Bay told the lady, "We'll take care of it, ma'am."

They walked up to the house and knocked. No answer. They went around to the back of the house and knocked. No answer. They went back to the front. The lady was watching them.

Bay announced, "We're going in the house to see if anything is wrong. It does smell around in back."

The elderly lady nodded. Bay got out his handy-dandy tool set and worked it around and the door lock clicked. When they opened the door, the stench nearly made them gag. Laryn got out her Vicks Vapor Rub and smeared it under her nose. She offered to share with Bay.

"I'll man it out," he said.

Laryn wanted to say, '*suit yourself*', but kept her mouth shut. Bay needed all his concentration to let his pea-brain work. She chided herself. Bay wasn't really a pea-brain, he just didn't tolerate women officers very well.

After a careful check downstairs they headed upstairs. The stench was stronger as they went up. Bay turned to her halfway up. "Maybe I'll take you up on your Vicks offer."

Laryn handed him her Vicks and then took it back, still not commenting on anything. They checked the two bedrooms before they had to tackle the closed bathroom door. Bay tried the handle. It wasn't locked, so he knocked first although they both figured no one would answer. Laryn took out her handkerchief. If she tossed her cookies, it had better be in her handkerchief rather than on the floor to complicate the investigation.

Bay swung the door wide. What they saw made even Bay swing around and lean his head against the hallway wall.

"What in the hell was that?" he asked Laryn.

Bay was a big guy, so Laryn's answer was, "You saw it better than I did. I'd guess it was a dead body."

"I think I'll call the coroner before we investigate any further."

"Can we go back outside? Maybe we could put up the yellow tape while we wait." Laryn wasn't sure how much longer her stomach would hold out.

"Sure, and we'll tell the neighbor lady what we might have found."

Outside the elderly lady wrung her hands as she waited. She walked closer to them.

"Ma'am, we think your neighbor might have expired in there. We'll know more when the coroner shows up."

"Oh, dear. I was afraid that might be it. I thought she might have visited someone, until I smelled the stench. I'll go in my house now. Thank you for coming so quickly, sir."

"It's our duty to serve you, ma'am. Take care now."

Laryn stared at Officer Bay Renaldo. This was a woman, admittedly old, but Bay was actually kind to her.

They put the yellow tape around the house. Laryn didn't want to think what they had to do when the coroner showed up. What little she saw in that bathroom made her want to vomit just thinking about it.

The coroner showed up along with another squad car. Officer Brunell got out of the squad car. Doctor Dennison, the coroner, got out of the other vehicle, all business and his black bag with him.

He looked at them, "What have we got here?"

Bay answered, "We think we have a dead body upstairs in the bathroom."

"You think, huh? Don't you know?"

Bay swung his arm and pointed towards the door. "Go see for yourself."

Doctor Dennison stiffly headed for the front door to the house followed by Officer Brunell. Bay touched Farley Brunell's arm. "You might want to put some Vicks under your nose. It's not pretty up there and it smells as bad."

"Thanks for the advice, but I'll tough it out."

Laryn shook her head. Were all men that stubborn that they couldn't use common sense when advised to use it? She followed the men. No one needed to protect the door or the yard. No one in their right mind would come in this house with that smell emanating from it

Before going in the bathroom, the coroner put on his gloves and a mask to keep from contaminating the scene. They all stood back while he opened the door. Laryn was at the back so got the full view of the object. It was grotesque. With the hair, she estimated that it was a woman with the blue gray eyes of the dead staring at them, encased by eyebrows on each side of her face. The woman must have been a large one and now had bloated to gigantic proportions. Her hands must have been on her lap, but were encased in her boobs. Her thighs were overlapping the toilet bowl and hung almost to the floor. The jowls on her face now hung down to where her boobs should be.

If they touched her would she explode?

The coroner turned to the officers. "Get her off the lavatory and place her on the floor."

They fellows looked at each other, then at Laryn. She answered for them. "Are you sure we can get her off that thing without her exploding?"

The coroner looked non plussed. "If she does, put her in the tub." He leaned down and closed the plug to the bathtub drain.

Shaking their heads the officers, reluctantly, put on gloves used for crime scenes.

Laryn asked, "Shouldn't we put some kind of clothes on her before we move her?"

The coroner looked at her as if she was out of her mind. "You could get a sheet if you want, otherwise nothing would fit over her in this condition."

Laryn gladly went looking for a sheet. When she came back with the sheet she recovered from the hall closet, the men were trying to get the woman off the toilet. She kind of slid like a bowl of Jello as they tried to lift her. They tried several other ways and angles, while the coroner just looked on with his hands on his hips.

Finally, Bay turned around to the man. "We need more help and I'd suggest the Fire Department. They have tools for just about any situation and I'd judge this as something we can't handle."

The coroner called the Fire Department. He explained the problem and told them to bring tools to take the toilet apart and a large body bag to hold the remains if it should start leaking.

In Laryn's mind she could see the expressions on the fire personnels' faces at that explanation. *Horror!*

The fire department came. This brought out half the neighborhood onto the street. The yellow tape kept them back. The firemen brought in a gurney, the body bag and tools. There was plenty of help now. Off the hook, Laryn and Farley traded off with Bay on going up to see what was going on.

They explained to the neighbors that their friend had died and they were trying to extract her from the house now. Laryn wondered how many of them might know what extract meant. Usually that meant in cuffs to extradite. This meant, however, that they would get the woman off the toilet. She didn't explain.

The Fire Department took the toilet apart and finally had to break it to get the woman's butt out of there. It had drooped down inside and her thighs had drooped outside so the poor toilet had been enclosed within her body.

When they brought her out, she was zipped in the body bag so her neighbors just hung their heads as she was taken away.

No trauma for them, thought Laryn, but this was her first dead body. She wouldn't get the first sight or the smell out of her mind for a long time and those open, sightless eyes would stare at her, at unexpected times, for quite awhile. The smell, however, she might never forget.

After work, she went home and showered extra long to get the imaginary smell off her and out of her nose.

ON AND OFF THE BEAT #8

The next day was a non-descript day, so after work Laryn went back to the Health Club. It was time to work her muscles a bit. Running maintained her stamina, but didn't work on her upper body building. She could use a bit of hyperventilating on Quinn's tight butt. Cripes! Butt made her think of the one they pulled out of the toilet yesterday. That one was not tight. It had been flabby to start with.

She checked in at the desk and went over to a machine that worked your arm and upper body parts. As she started to work the machine, she looked around the area to try to spot Quinn. He wasn't visible right now, so she worked harder pulling her arms together and working her stomach muscles. She must need the workout as she was starting to perspire.

She stopped to drink from her water container. If you perspire, you need to re-hydrate. You could faint from dehydration just as easily in a Health Club as on a hiking trail if you didn't drink enough water, Dave Dunlap had told her that. As she was sipping, Quinn walked in from some inner sanctum, probably his office, to peruse the crowd.

Man, he looked good. He had on a muscleman sleeveless shirt that showed off his upper body to perfection. Drool, drool, thought Laryn.

He looked around and smiled when he spotted Laryn. He came over and stood in front of her, arms crossed. "I knew something had happened in here. The building suddenly seemed charged with energy." He turned, cocking his head slightly. "It was probably those guys ogling you." He moved a little to one side to take her out of their line of sight.

"Hey, big guy, I can take care of myself, you know." She huffed a little while she talked mainly because she was winded from working the upper body machine.

Okay, she thought. Honestly, I'm winded because a good-looking guy came up to me with his muscles bulging from crossing them in front of my eyes.

"Done anymore wildlife viewing since I saw you?"

Laryn eyed him. Was he jealous of Dave? It had only been a few days since they had eaten dinner at her mother's. "No wildlife viewing until I came in here, but will a dead body do?"

Quinn blinked at that. He had forgotten that those things were part of her job. He'd seen his share of dead bodies during his days in the Marines. "I'm sorry, Laryn, I shouldn't have brought up your work day. I know you come in here not only to work your body, but to get the job out of your mind for an hour or so." He leaned in and put his hands next to hers on the bar. "I'm sorry!"

She almost leaned into him, but that would have put her forehead against his. That would be a no-no at the Health Club, so she stared into his blue eyes. "You couldn't know about the dead body. It was something that I'll have a hard time forgetting, but it's just part of the service we provide for our taxpayers. Sometime I might tell you about it," she grinned, "but not at my mom's house. It's not dinner time conversation."

He took one hand off the bar and a step back. "After I get off work, could I take you out for a drink or something to get your mind off your work? I've eaten so much at your folk's house, the least I can do is take their daughter out for a dinner or a drink."

"So you'll only take me out to pay back my mother?"

His cheeks turned a little red. "I didn't mean it like that. You're fun to talk to and your body is beautiful to look at. Those yahoos behind me know what I'm talking about and I feel I'd better make time before they get over here and become my competition."

She raised her eyebrows while still working her arms. "Oh, so I'm just another game to be won for you."

He shook his head. "I'm not going to win verbally with you, am I?"

She laughed. "I'm just jerking your chain, Quinn. Why don't you come up to my apartment when you get off work and I'll treat you to home squeezed lemonade. I could even make you a sandwich if you're hungry. We could just watch a movie or talk if you'd rather."

"I think that would be great, but I'll bring a vegetarian pizza for a snack to go with the lemonade. We can talk between commercials."

"Sounds like fun to me. I'll get off this machine, shower and go home and make the drink. See you after nine."

Laryn bounced off her machine and quickly hit the showers, then went to the store to get lemons to make the lemonade. Thank God ice and water were readily available.

Quinn showed up at her door about nine thirty. H waved a pizza under her nose and walked over to her table to plunk it down. He put his hands on his hips as he looked around. Her apartment was very eclectic; retro table and chairs, modern electric stove, dishwasher and refrigerator. The couch was an old camel back long one done in a brown material with a matching chair. The couch had a hand knit throw in bright colors draped over the back corner with some pillows in yellow satin. One chair was a dark green recliner and probably vinyl. He hated his vinyl chair when he had shorts on. It stuck to his legs.

He smiled at her. "Hi, beautiful, ready to eat?"

She shut the door, still in shock after he walked right past her to put the pizza on the table without saying a word.

"Hi yourself. You walked right by me. What if this was the wrong apartment and you just breezed right on in? I'd be without a pizza and you'd be without lemon juice and in the wrong place. I'm sure whoever it was would accept the pizza and probably pay you for it, then show you the door."

He looked surprised. "Are you mad at me?"

"No, but a girl has to be on her toes when she answers the door. You're lucky I didn't trip you, take you down to the floor and cuff you."

He laughed, "Go ahead and cuff me. I don't usually play games like that, but what-the-hey, I'm up to any challenge."

He looked so good in his white stiff shirt with rolled up cuffs and tight jeans. Tight, tight jeans!

"Oh, go on with you, as Mom always says." She reached into the cupboard and brought down two glasses, filling them with ice from her icemaker door spout. Opening the fridge, she poured the glasses full of lemonade and set them on the table. Reaching around, she brought her napkins in the holder and set it on the table.

"Sit down, dinner is served."

Quinn sat down and put a napkin on his lap. "I should put this around my neck when I eat pizza, but I'm in the company of a lady, so I'll put it on my lap."

"You'd do better at putting it under your glass. They're old and sweat with cold stuff in them. They'll dribble all down your shirt when you drink out of them."

Quinn looked at his glass. It had Disney's Goofy imprinted on it. "You think I'm Goofy?"

"No, but would you rather have my glass with Mickey Mouse and Minnie on it? How about the heart between them? Kind of cute don't you think?" She perused her glass, turning it around and around so he could get the full view.

He laughed, "So your mother uses real crystal and you use Disney glasses? I kind of like these Disney glasses. I'm always afraid of breaking your mother's"

She snorted. "Ha! You break mine and you've broken an antique glass."

His eyes widened. "You're kidding, right?"

She laughed. "Mom gave me these when I moved in here. She got these when she was a kid from some promotion that one of the fast food places had. They lasted through her childhood, then, Dayne's and mine. She didn't think of them as worth anything, so I got them. I'm kind of clumsy in the kitchen." She bowed her head.

Quinn opened the pizza box and proceeded to take out a piece. "Here, have a slice and get your mind off your problems. No one can eat a pizza and think of troubles. Pizza is a happy meal."

She scrunched her nose at him and grabbed a piece. Vegetarian might not be her thing, but this was good, spicy and flavorful. "At ten o'clock I'll turn on one of my favorite blood and guts shows to watch until the news comes on at eleven. After that, I go to bed, so I can fight crime and corruption in real life tomorrow."

"Yeah, and I need to rest up so I can keep the Health Club going to keep those bodies in shape to fight that crime and corruption."

Laryn smiled, "Sometimes yours is crime and punishment for your clientele."

He nodded, "Only those that don't appreciate a firm body."

She secretly smirked, "Oh, I appreciate a firm body. I especially like it when I look around your place. All those firm, tight-ended, backsides. Wow!"

Quinn's ears turned color. "Okay, knock it off. I've tried to keep those guys off you down there and this is the thanks I get. You peruse their bodies?"

"Yup, and I won't apologize either. Grab your drink. We need to watch my show."

Her apartment was very compact. She plopped down on the end of the couch facing the TV. That left him with the other end, or a chair. He chose the other end as it would be easier to view the TV program. The vinyl recliner looked to be her reading chair. Laryn pulled the coffee table up against the couch to put their drinks on. She had the controls in her hand and selected the channel she wanted and turned to him.

"I'll make us a bag of microwave popcorn as soon as the show starts."

"That's okay. I've taken the last slice of the pizza and a napkin to put it on."

Quinn noticed her fish bowl on top of the hutch she had her TV in. As he watched, they didn't move. "Are your fish alive or are they just sleeping. I haven't seen them move while the commercial was on."

Laryn laughed, "Go over and stick your finger in the bowl. Maybe that will wake them up."

Quinn got up and took the few steps to the hutch. Looking in he saw only water. Turning back to her, he said, "There's only water in the bowl. But the fish look so real from the couch."

"I know. Mom knows I forget to feed the fish and water my plants, so she found this bowl that looks like it has fish in it. The Ivy plant lives in the water, too, so I only have to water it when it gets low. I change the water in the fish bowl and water the Ivy at the same time, like once a month or when the water starts to grow green slime. Mom says it makes the place look lived in and the plant sucks up bad air quality and spews out the good stuff."

Sitting back down, Quinn nodded, "Smart lady, your mother." To himself he thought, *green slime?*

The show started and at the next commercial, she made the popcorn and brought it back to munch on and refilled their lemonade glasses.

When the show finished, Quinn got up to leave. At the door, he thanked her for the enjoyable evening, then reached over and grabbed her arm slowly pulling her towards him. He leaned in and kissed her surprised mouth, at the action. It tasted of popcorn. Yum!

"Goodnight, lovely lady," and he left grinning to himself. The kiss felt great to him even though he had surprised her. Next time he'd improve the delivery with her cooperation. He could hardly wait.

Laryn slowly closed the door and locked it. She was still in shock. Tight-buns Quinn had kissed her. She took that delightful thought to bed with her. Her dreams took an erotic turn from this point on.

The next day Laryn came home to a message on her answering machine. *"Miz. Scott. This is Feliz Toreno. I called the Sheriff's Department like you asked me to. Now they harass me about my daughter. They think I'm the one who made her run away. They check my house today. Tomorrow they are going to check my property. Can you come help me explain to them about Maya? Please come."*

Laryn's hands cupped her cheeks. "Lord, what did I do to poor Feliz? They think he might of have had a hand in her disappearance." She stomped around her tiny apartment and then looked out the window towards the slow moving river. The better to think out her thoughts as she studied a bobbing glob of something.

She could take off tomorrow to help Mr. Toreno. She could explain to the sheriff why they were worried. Mr. Toreno didn't deserve this harassment. He was as concerned as she was about the disappearance of Maya.

Laryn called the Police Department and requested the day off for personal reasons. She said she could be on call if they needed her. Just call her cell phone. Harve, on the night desk, said he would write the message down and get it to the right person.

Good. That was taken care off. Now to call Mr. Toreno. He answered on the second ring. "Mr. Toreno, this is Laryn Scott. I'm calling as a friend of Maya's. Yes, I'll come to your house and explain about the call I got from someone and I thought it might be Maya."

"I am so glad, Miz Scott, that you will come. I'm afraid of the policia. In Mexico, they no listen very well until you are locked up and then they talk to you. My animals will need me."

"What time do you want me to be at your house?"

"I no know. They just said tomorrow with a warrant to search."

"Could you just call me when they arrive? It isn't that far out to your house and I could be there within ten minutes."

"I will do that, Miz Scott and I thank you so much. I'm afraid for my Maya and for myself."

"Take care, Mr. Toreno. Until tomorrow when I'll see you. Bye for now."

"Gracias. Adios." Clearly Mr. Toreno was upset. He had reverted back to his native tongue, thought Laryn.

ON AND OFF THE BEAT #9

Laryn was waiting by the phone for Feliz's call. She hadn't done her run in the fear she would miss it. She had instead cooked a hardy meal of bacon, eggs and whole wheat toast. Her mother's raspberry jam was so good with this toast. If she'd had to leave it, she would have eaten it for supper. That was what microwaves were for.

Feliz's call came at nine o'clock. The policia were there and he didn't know what to do.

"I'll be there in ten minutes, Mr. Toreno. Just stay on your porch until I get there. Let them do their job. It will look better if we don't worry about what they will find. You have nothing to hide."

"Si, senorita, I have nothing to hide."

Laryn made it to the Toreno house in the ten minutes she had promised him. He was standing hunched over wringing his hands.

One squad car was there and she could see two officers perusing the grounds. When they saw her pull up, the officers came back to question her. They introduced themselves as Detective Fenton and Detective Smith. Smith was a woman. Laryn appreciated that information as the woman officer might understand about hunches.

"I'm Laryn Scott. I work for the Mount Vernon police department, but that has very little to do with this case."

"Mr. Toreno said you know more than he does about the disappearance of his daughter."

"Yes I do." And she went on to explain how a telephone call on her answering machine had triggered a hunch who this caller might have been. "I still don't know if, in fact, it really was Maya Toreno who called me, but she hasn't shown up yet, nor has Mr. Toreno or myself heard from her. I believe that would be about five weeks now."

After a little more of reiterating the facts, they proceeded to go on with their searching the property.

"May we follow you around? We won't get in your way, but if you have any questions, we'll be right there to answer them if we can."

Mr. Toreno nodded his head, but seemed too frightened to speak. The investigators started looking the flower beds over for freshly turned ground. Nothing. There was a hug patch of Evergreen blackberry vines just across the fence of the neatly groomed yard. They search that with long poles they had for probing water. Nothing. The two officers were very thorough and dogmatic in their search. They made it back to the barn area.

Laryn knew this would be hard to search as the cattle would have kept the dirt churned up. That pig farmer in Canada had used that fact to his advantage until human bones had appeared and triggered additional searching. However, the detectives opened the gate and checked the ground. Even churned up, it was hard underneath and would feel different if a hole had been dug. Laryn knew this from some of the training classes she had attended. She watched them search, learning first hand how this was done.

The detectives tackled the barn next. It was as neat as the rest of Mr. Toreno's holdings. They might be old, but he had kept them up, plus worked another farm for pay as well. The old fellow was a hard worker.

Now, other than the hay rolls and the stacked alfalfa bales, the rest of the place was fields with cattle in them. The detectives would just have to hike it, or check it out with a helicopter. They even might bring out cadaver dogs. God, she hated to think they would have to go that far.

At this point, she hoped that Maya was happy and well living in California, sun tanning on the beach and swimming in the ocean or even waiting tables in a bar-side barista. Laryn smiled at her happy thoughts for Maya.

The hay bales, wrapped in heavy white plastic, were out closer to the fence line and had a wide gate for a tractor to go through. The hay was probably to feed the cattle out in the pasture. The alfalfa was in a lean-to beside the barn. It needed cover or it would get wet since it was just baled and not incased in white plastic.

The detectives discussed something between the two of them and headed for the alfalfa shed. As they got closer, Laryn was getting whiffs of a distinctive odor. She had smelled something just like this odor only days ago. Her heart began to pound. She stopped and looked at Mr. Toreno. He seemed unconcerned.

"Mr. Toreno, have any of your animals died recently?

He shook his head. "No. Why do you ask?"

"The smell is like rotting flesh."

"Ah, that is because some of the alfalfa is rotting on the bottom and it smells like manure."

Laryn shook her head. "Does it always smell this bad?"

Feliz thought a minute. "No, it usually smells sickening sweet. I never think about it anymore."

"Would you wait here while I go talk to the detectives. I'm a little worried right now, but I don't want you to worry, so stay right here if you will."

His eyes widened. Of course he looked worried, but he nodded and acted like he was glued to the ground.

Laryn walked over to the detectives. "I just talked to Mr. Toreno and he said the smell you are experiencing is from alfalfa rotting on the bottom. He still is innocent as far as I'm concerned, but I just came off of a case where the lady had died in her bathroom and the smell was much like what I'm smelling right now."

Detectives Smith and Fenten looked at Laryn, neither smiling. Detective Fenten nodded at Laryn. "You might have called it to our attention, but we agree, it didn't smell right to us either and we were just going to talk to the fellow about it. We'll probably bring in the cadaver dogs before we have to move the alfalfa."

Laryn looked concerned. "Please don't accuse him of anything. He's scared enough already. He said the police in Mexico take you to jail and then question you. He is terrified that that will happen here. He's worried that no one would take care of his animals if that happened. He knows he's done nothing to Maya. He is just worried about her."

"We'll be discrete in asking if we can remove the alfalfa bales to another area."

"Thank you for that and I agree that the alfalfa must be moved."

Laryn was shaking her head as she approached Mr. Toreno. "They have to get a crew in to move the alfalfa. Can you tell them where to put it and arrange a cover so it will keep dry?"

"Si, I can do that. I'll get some blue tarps to put over it with tie-downs for the wind."

"They may be bringing in some dogs to sniff around. They won't let them loose, so you don't have to worry that they will chase your cattle."

Nodding his head, he agreed, "Gracious, I would worry."

"Let's go back to the house while the detectives do their job and you can go get the tarps to put over the alfalfa."

Feliz nodded again, "I will need to go to a hardware store for the supplies."

"You go and I'll stay here until the detectives leave or you get back. Will that be all right?"

"Si, I will get my keys." He went inside his home and returned almost immediately. He left in his older, but heavy duty truck.

Detectives Fenton and Smith came over to confer with Laryn.

"We'll come back tomorrow after we get everything arranged. I don't think there will be any hurry to find out what our next search will find." He turned and looked at Detective Smith, "Don't you agree?"

"I'm sorry to say, but yes I agree." Detective Smith shook her head and looked down-cast.

Laryn nodded, "I'll come back tomorrow to support Mr. Toreno on what you might find under the alfalfa."

The detectives left. Laryn waited for Mr. Toreno to come back. When he did, Laryn explained the situation to him. She felt he didn't have a clue on what they might find, only that they would move the alfalfa.

She left to go home. Her heart was sad. She felt she knew what was under the alfalfa, but not what might have happened to Maya to put her under that pile. Maya was supposed to be in California in a sunny place enjoying herself, not in a dark place that she would never return from.

ON AND OFF THE BEAT #10

Laryn arranged another day off. She showed up at the Toreno house at nine o'clock. That seemed to be the time the police decided they could safely be at homes and not look invasive. You weren't met at the door with a rifle and a sleepy person holding it.

It was only a few minutes later the patrol car showed up followed by a van. Detectives Fenton and Smith got out of the patrol car. They walked back to the van, converse with the driver, then left to approach Laryn and Feliz. After the usual good mornings and hand shakes. Detective Fenton explained.

"Mr. Toreno, we will let the dog sniff the area and determine if we need to move the alfalfa. Then if the dog acts agitated, we will get the team that is on stand-by to come out and move the alfalfa to an area you have selected."

"Si, sir. I have the tarps to put over it now, too. Can we keep it close to the barn, so I don't have to pack my alfalfa so far for my cattle?"

"Yes, I think we can do that. It just needs to be moved out from under the lean-to. If we find nothing there, you can move it back under the lean-to at your leisure."

Feliz looked at Laryn in confusion, "Leisure?"

Laryn explained, "He means when you can find time, you may move it back under the lean-to."

Feliz nodded his head, "Si."

"I think we'd be wise to stay on the porch and let them do their job." Laryn didn't want Mr. Toreno to get the first glimpse of what they might find with the cadaver dog.

The detectives went back to the van. Another officer got out and released a huge German Shepard. They clipped a leash on him and started for the hay baled in white plastic wrap. The dog gave them a merry chase and Laryn and Feliz grinned at each other over the antics of the dog. In Laryn's mind it

---

67

was interesting to note the dog's hind legs were always at a crouched position making it ready to spring forward at a moments notice.

When they finished the white-wrapped bales, they took the dog over to the corral and let it sniff around. At the rate the dog did his job, this would be over shortly. Then it was time for the alfalfa shed. This was the part Laryn dreaded. She watched the dog stop and hold its head up. If it had been a hunting dog you would think it was on point. It looked at its trainer, ready, willing and able to tackle the next job.

The officer nodded to the dog. The dog jerked forward, nearly pulling the officers' arms out of their sockets. The dog whined, running to and fro systematically from one end to the other of the alfalfa bales. Finally it stopped about the middle of the stack, sat down and stared at the bales. Its body quivered with knowledge. The handler called the dog off and gave it some kind of treat. The dog swallowed the treat and stood at attention facing the alfalfa shed.

There was a conference among the officers and finally Detective Fenton came over to talk to Laryn and Feliz.

"We feel there is enough evidence with the dog sniffing to move the alfalfa. Could you tell us where you would like the bales to be put, Mr. Toreno?"

Feliz looked worriedly at Laryn. She nodded. Then he nodded at the officer and without a word, slowly went over to tell them where to pile the alfalfa. Laryn dragging her feet brought up the rear. Feliz gestured about three feet out from the lean-to, still without speaking. The officers nodded and one got on a cell phone to arrange the move. Detective Smith must have radioed the station while he did that. Laryn noticed both seemed to be talking to someone.

The dog handler came over and spoke to Laryn and Feliz. Laryn felt the officer didn't know if Feliz spoke English at this point. The dog stood at his side but sniffed in the direction of both Laryn and Feliz.

"Mr. Toreno and Ms. Scott, I'll take the dog back to his pen for now. If we are needed later, we'll come back." He smiled then. "If we stayed here, it would be like keeping track of a child, and a nosey child at that."

His smile seemed to relax Feliz, and he smiled back. "Thank you for your help, Officer."

"No trouble. It helps to keep the dog on track to work him once in a while." He left, put the dog in the van and drove away.

Laryn didn't know what to do with Feliz until the alfalfa was moved. "Do you have anything you need to do? It may take awhile to get all this organized and the alfalfa moved."

Feliz thought a minute. "I could mow the grass. It will save me time later in the week."

"Good idea. I'll go over and sit here on the porch while you do your work and wait until the officers are through."

"You are too kind, Miz. Scott. I'll get you some iced tea and some biscuits I made this morning."

Laryn grinned at him, "No you are the one that is too kind. I loved your biscuits last time I came."

She sat in his rocker on the porch while he rode his lawn mower around. Mean while some fellows came to restack the alfalfa. The officers stood back and watched. They took some pictures and talked periodically on their radios that squawked and crackled.

One fellow came over and asked Laryn if Mr. Toreno would like the damp alfalfa put in a separate pile.

"The stench is pretty bad and may rot more of the alfalfa if put on top of the rest."

Laryn answered for Mr. Toreno. "I think that would be best. He can't afford to lose more of his feed. He can put it back on the bottom when he restacks the bales. Thank you for the thought"

Detective Smith came over to Laryn. "It smells terrible over there. We'll be digging around the area. Please keep Mr. Toreno away until we're through. It's for his benefit I'm asking this of you." She shook her head in denial at Laryn. "It doesn't look good."

"I was afraid of that when I smelled it the first time. Maya wasn't my best friend, but I really liked her and after helping Mr. Toreno with the investigation, I think he is a loving and caring father for his only child."

"If she's under there, this will be so sad for him. Do you have any idea on what might have happened here?"

Laryn shook her head. "I only know what I heard on my answering machine. My off-the-clock investigation tells me there was a boy friend trucker that she was supposed to go on the road with for a vacation of some kind. Mr. Toreno only knows what I know."

Detective Smith went back to the operation area. Feliz had finished his mowing and returned his mower to the garage and came back to where Laryn was sitting.

"How is the detective's investigation going? I see they are digging around in the dirt."

Laryn felt sad. She needed to prepare Feliz for what the detectives thought they would find. "Mr. Toreno, the detectives think they might have found a clue in the disappearance of Maya. You must prepare yourself in case it's bad news."

"No! No! Miz Scott. It can't be bad news. My Maya is all I have. She is my world that I work and breathe for." He wiped his eyes and sat down on the porch steps. "I will not believe this."

They watched from the porch as the detectives put the yellow tape up around the crime scene. To Laryn, it was now official. There had been a crime committed and when the detectives came over to tell them what they had found, they would all know what they were dealing with.

The detectives came slowly over to the waiting couple. They had two bags with them and a camera case was slung over the shoulder of Detective Smith.

Detective Fenton seemed to be in charge again. "Mr. Toreno, is this your daughter's cell phone?"

Feliz shook his head in denial. "It could be. I don't know. They all look alike to me."

Detective Smith pulled the very dirty overnight bag out of the plastic bag. "Sir, is this your daughter's suitcase?"

Feliz's hands shook as he wrung them. "Si, it looks like hers, but hers should be with her on her vacation. That one is very dirty. Maya would never take that one."

Fenton looked at the old guy. Toreno did seem to be confused. However, he was an officer of the law and had to follow procedures. "We're going to have to ask you to come over to courthouse and give a statement." He shook his head. "There is a body over there and it has to be processed before we know what happened, but meanwhile we need to question you on what you know."

Feliz turned to Laryn, tears streaming down his face. "Madre de Dios!" He made the sign of the cross. "Miz Scott, what they are saying?"

She held out her arms to him. As he came to her, she held his arms with her hands, looking him in his watery eyes and saying, "He is saying that they think it might be Maya. We must prepare ourselves for the worst and hope for the best."

He came the rest of the way into her arms. She held him as he sobbed, looking sadly at the officers. "This is so hard for both of us."

They nodded. "We need to ask you to come down, too, and make a statement."

"Of course I will and I'll bring Mr. Toreno with me. He shouldn't be alone right now."

Feliz looked up at Laryn. "Can I go see if that is my daughter?"

Detective Fenton answered for Laryn. "I don't think that is a good idea. You can't see much and we need to have the coroner here and then the forensic people will determine what may have happened."

"When will I know if that is my daughter?"

"When we know, you'll know. That's the best we can do for now. Just be prepared, Mr. Toreno." The detective patted the old guy on the back

An ambulance came. The detectives pointed their fingers in the direction of the barn and lean-to. They oversaw the removal of the body. Laryn and Feliz couldn't see anything as the ambulance was blocking their view.

It was just as well, thought Laryn. She didn't need to see this anymore than Feliz did. When the ambulance left, the officers motioned for Laryn to follow. She asked Feliz to ride with her. They got in her car and followed the police cruiser to their office in the courthouse in Mount Vernon.

ON AND OFF THE BEAT #11

Laryn and Feliz were shown into a room. When Detective Fenton came in, he asked Laryn to wait outside the room while he talked to Mr. Toreno. She knew this would happen, so wasn't surprised by the request.

Finally, Feliz came out and Fenton asked Laryn to step in. She only answered the questions he asked. She felt the investigative work she had done shouldn't lead them on the wrong trail or influence their investigation. If they asked her, she would tell them what she had found out, which wasn't very much. Evan she knew that.

The detectives asked Feliz not to leave town and knew the place he worked, if they couldn't find him at home. He moved up close to Laryn and looked at the detectives.

"You think I would kill my daughter, the only thing I have in this world? If you tell where I work that, I will lose my job. I cannot live on my farm alone. I did not kill anyone. I have not even hurt anyone in my life." His eyes begged them to understand.

Detective Fenton hoped his emotions didn't show. He believed Mr. Toreno, but the investigation must proceed along guidelines, so as not to compromise the investigation. After all, this looked like a murder scene. "Sir, we will not tell anyone about your daughter. It will come out that she is missing. That might bring someone forward who might have information we can use to find your missing daughter. We don't know yet if the body is your daughter. But it is a body and we must investigate it as such."

Feliz nodded, "Si, I understand. Gracias."

Laryn took Feliz home. "Will you be all right here alone, Mr. Toreno?"

"Si. I will fix my comida." He looked at her and translated, "Dinner."

Laryn patted him on the shoulder. "Good. If you need someone to talk to, be sure and call me." She looked over at the area where the body was found. It still had the yellow tape around it. "You won't be able to move your alfalfa back in the lean-to yet. When they remove the yellow ribbon, they will probably let you move it then."

He nodded and got out of her car. She left to go home. A long run and a shower would help her. She felt dirty just thinking about the dead body under Feliz' alfalfa pile.

During the next two weeks, Laryn called Mr. Toreno every other day. She did patrol rides with Officer Brunnell and bad-ass, Officer Renaldo.

Sunday dinners at her parents home was a nice break as Dayne and Quinn Madden, the hunk, was there. They shot baskets and she managed to bump Quinn whenever she could, rubbing her butt against his leg as she held out her arm to keep him from swatting the ball away as she dribbled.

Dayne had the audacity to call a personal foul on her when she leaned over Quinn's back to swat the ball out of his hands. So she had rubbed her boobs over the guy's back, so what! She had felt his muscles on his arms, too. It made up for the two points Quinn got for the foul.

When she had Sundays off, the dinners at her family' home and Quinn, made her week seem better when she couldn't get to the Health Club to ogle the muscular bodies.

She also found out that Dayne had a game in eastern Washington His second string team would be playing Liberty Bell just for practice.

In her investigation of the reverse directory for the telephone company, Maya had put in a call to a phone number over there. It would give Laryn an excuse to talk to Bubba or his family on what they knew about Maya. The investigative team hadn't called her yet, so she felt she could do this and plead innocent of knowledge about the case if it came to murder.

"Can I go with you to Liberty Bell? I'd love to see a game."

Dayne looked at her as if she was crazy. "Sure, but you'll have to take your car. You can't ride with the team. Insurance problems, you know."

Laryn smiled. "I kind of knew that." She turned to Quinn. "Do you want to go?"

"I am going, but I get to ride the bus." He shook his head and pursed his lips. "Lucky me."

Dayne laughed, "Hey man, you'll get to hear the newest kid-jokes. It might be a little hard to understand them for an old codger like you."

"Hey man, I'm not much older than you, but it is true that I hear more dirty jokes than clean."

That led to talk about birthdays and age. Laryn found out that she was the old codger here. She was six months older than Quinn. He was about nine months older than Dayne. He'd gone straight into the Marines after

---

high school and had taken a lot of medical courses to work with the wounded trauma cases. When he'd gotten out he had a course in management. Now he managed a Health Club.

That made sense to Laryn. She asked him, "Do you have a family?"

"No, I really don't. Down in California, my family was really screwed up. We went back and forth between our mother and foster homes. I wasn't sure who were my sisters or brothers. I think my mother would take over some man's family and he would leave her with them and then we'd all be taken away from her for awhile, but eventually returned. Maybe, she was a foster mother, too, for all I know."

Laryn was horrified at the life Quinn had led. "Do you know where anybody is now?"

He shook his head. "No. I wrote a few letters, but some were returned finally. I didn't bother to investigate where anyone was when I got out of the service. I truly didn't care, sad as that sounds."

After that revelation, Laryn thought they should change the subject. It wasn't long until she left for her apartment down by the river. She'd change the water in her fish bowl and add water to her ivy plant.

The trip to eastern Washington was beautiful. The fall colors were starting to come into play with orange and yellows against the evergreen trees. The sky was bright blue with cumulus clouds floating on high. She could pick out a cloud shaped like a dragon chasing a running dog which was turning into a girl with curly hair. Another couple turns showed round hay bales in pastures ready to be taken to areas as winter food for animals. A herd of deer was back near a wooded area. She'd seen more wildlife this year than she had in most of her life.

She went through the little western town of Winthrop and on to the next town.

Instead of going to the school, she had programmed her GPS unit to the address she had from the reverse directory of the phone company. Laryn progressed into a rural area. More hay fields appeared. Rolling hills backed most of the farms. If you weren't intimidated by the lack of shopping malls, this was nice, peaceful and smelled of fresh air, sunshine and fresh cut hay.

Laryn slowed down. The number on the mailbox and the GPS unit said she would turn left in about a half a mile. She could see a standard two story house, painted white. As she neared, she saw a flatbed semi-truck parked towards the back.

Wow! Would she be able to interview Bubba? That was not a good idea. He could lie, plus his wife would be intimidated by him being there. She wondered if she should try the criminal version of casing the place by knocking on the door and asking directions to someplace if someone answered.

Nothing ventured, nothing gained. She parked and went to the door. A woman about Laryn's own age answered.

"Yes, what do you want?" The lady didn't act too friendly.

"My name is Laryn Scott. I see you have a truck able to deliver hay or alfalfa. Is it for hire?"

The lady made a face. "It would be if that no-good son-of-a-bitch ever came home to drive it again."

"What do you mean? He's not home?" Laryn was confused. Where was the man?

"When he came back from the California trip, he parked the truck, worked on the motor for awhile and then disappeared. I haven't seen him since."

"Good heavens, how long ago was that?"

"That was about three months ago. I'm about ready to sell the truck to get some money to live on. My waitress job just barely keeps us going. Ya wanta buy a truck?"

Laryn was taken back. This poor woman must be hungry for companionship or she wouldn't have opened up so freely with her, thought Laryn. "No. My friend in Mount Vernon hired a load of alfalfa to be delivered and I thought your husband was the one to deliver it."

She put her hands on her hips, "No, my husband's last delivery was a load of hay, but I'll bet your friend is the bitch that called here and told me my Bubba was going to pick her up for a trip and she was ready and waiting. I told her off and then called my Denny and told him off, too. If he took a woman on a trip, he could just not bother coming home either."

"Your husband's name is Denny, not Bubba?"

The woman looked confused for a minute. "You're right. His name is Denny and not Bubba. I've had other drivers call here and ask for Denny, so I think that is the only name he goes by. Maybe your friend dialed the wrong number."

Laryn smiled even though she was as confused as the woman. "Could be. This guy, Bubba, might be giving out the number of guys he knows so he won't get into trouble with his wife."

That stopped the woman for a second. "That jerk! I'll bet that is what happened. I know the fellows do stupid things like that. I know Denny thought that was funny. He mentioned something like that about a guy and thought it was hilarious. I told him I thought it was stupid, but you know men?" She shrugged her shoulders.

Laryn shook her head. "Not really, but I work with fellows that think something is funny when it really isn't."

By now, it was like talking to a friend.

The woman, Mrs. Anderson, asked Laryn. "I'd like to ask a favor of you. You're the first woman to show up here and I'm afraid to ask a man, but would you go up to the upper barn with me? There was said to be a cougar hanging around the farms here and I'm afraid to go up there to check on the horse we have. My daughter, who is at school, is worried. We haven't seen it or Denny for about three months. Awful smells have come down the canyon in the evening when the wind blows. The cougar could have gotten the horse. I'd like to know before my daughter gets home."

"Sure, Mrs. Anderson. Let me go to my car to get a weapon."

The woman grabbed her chest. "You have a weapon?" She made a motion to close the door.

Laryn raised her hand like she was going to surrender. "In my job, I'm a police officer. I'm over here with my brother who is a coach with his team. I was just doing a favor for a friend when I came to your house. I feel a gun would be useful for going up a canyon where a cougar might be living. I keep it in a locked strong box in the trunk of my car."

The woman pushed her door open again. "Man. You gave me a start. I'm not much for guns, but I'd use one if I had to. I'll get my coat and let's go. I'll come out the back door."

Laryn nodded, went to her car for the gun and then walked around to the back door of the house. In just a few minutes, Mrs. Anderson came out to lead Laryn up the canyon. The going was good as there was a wagon trail to take food up to the animals that might live in the barn. Mrs. Anderson clutched her coat to her chest even though the day wasn't that cold, just breezy. Laryn could smell an odd smell, but if something happened three months ago, nature would have handled most of the carnage.

Looking over the fence on the back side of the barn, they discovered the mangled mess of a dead animal that had mostly dried up. It looked like it had been fodder for a lot of different wildlife as pieces of it were strewn around the area and many pieces were missing.

"Oh, yuck! Do you think it's our horse? My daughter is going to be so upset if it is." Her white, stricken face looked over at Laryn. "Could we check the barn for the cougar? I can't let my daughter come up here unless I know the cougar is long gone."

"Sure, Mrs. Anderson. I'll go in first. I'll treat it like a suspect. My gun won't be of much use to shoot a cougar, but it can scare it."

"I'll go to the front of the barn and you can leave the back door open so it can escape. That is, if it is in there."

"Good idea." Laryn went inside the fence. She slowly approached the door that was half hanging from its hinges. It was the one used to let the animals out into the pasture. The front of the barn had the double doors. The strange odor was in there, too.

As she approached the door, there was a loud explosion as the door hit the side of the barn and the horse raced through the carnage and up the hill as if the cougar was on its trail. Laryn's heart was nearly choking her from the fright.

"Are you all right in there?" Mrs. Anderson called out.

"Yeah. You don't need to worry about the horse. It's still running and may be hard to woo back. Don't come in as I haven't checked out the inside of the barn yet."

Laryn sidled up to the door again with her heart racing and her gun hand shaking. With her back against the wall where the door opened, she let her eyes adjust to the darkened barn

As she listened, there didn't seem to be a noise of any kind. Stepping into the barn the dust motes sparkled in the few rays of light filtering through the slits in the wooden shakes on the roof. It smelled of hay and maybe a little horse poop. Slowly her eyes adjusted to the semi-darkness.

There in front of her, over by the stalls was a sight she didn't know if she was seeing correctly. She knew Mrs. Anderson shouldn't come in until she figured it out.

She yelled out, "Mrs. Anderson, don't come in here. There doesn't seem to be a cougar in here, but I'm not sure what else is here."

Laryn walked over to see what the object was. There in the dim light was a cadaver. It was hanging from a rope that led up into the hay loft. Its shoes were missing, but the feet were touching the floor. What was strange was its skin had dried to leather and its neck had stretched to about two feet long. Her immediate thought was of the old west neck-stretching. Did that really happen? She was torn between throwing up and laughing. The laughing might be from shock.

Laryn checked the details of the cadaver, while its dead eyes stared at her. The rope was twisted around its neck but was not in a knot. A pitchfork was close by its feet with dried dark stuff on it which could have been blood. The pants were hanging low, the shirt almost off its shoulders. Looking around she spotted the shoes. They looked like they had been flipped around the barn, and again, oh God, that stretched neck with a mouth nearly pulled up into its nose. It had what looked like red hair. Now, that was distinctive, thought Laryn. She went to the front of the barn and squeezed through the door, not letting Mrs. Anderson see what was inside.

Still shaking, she told Mrs. Anderson, "I don't want you to see what I've found in there. The cougar wasn't there, but I found something strange."

"What is it Ms. Scott?"

"I think it might be a body."

Mrs. Anderson looked stricken. "You don't think it might be my husband do you?"

Laryn shook her head. "I'm not sure. What color was your husband's hair?"

The breathless voice said, "Red."

Laryn put her arm around the lady. "It looked red to me, but I could be wrong in the dull light."

Mrs. Anderson made like she was going in the barn to see what was there. Laryn stopped her. "I think we'd do better to call 911 and let them decide what to do."

"What will I tell them?" She looked confused and disoriented.

"I'll talk to them if you'd like me to. I'll have to stick around until they show up as I found whatever it is that's in the barn."

At almost a whisper Mrs. Anderson said, "I'll appreciate that."

Laryn felt like the woman next to her had shrunk and turned into an old lady while she watched. Her coat was pulled tight around her and she kind of bent over as they walked. Laryn held her arm lightly and felt she might blow away if Laryn wasn't holding on to her.

With vacant eyes, Mrs. Anderson looked at Laryn. "The horse was okay?"

Laryn quietly reassured her. "Yes, but it might be hard to convince it to come back to the barn. That was a lot for a sensitive horse to handle."

When they got to the house, Laryn made the call, but only said she thought they had found a body, but it had been dead, according to her calculations, about three months.

Since it wasn't an emergency, they told her it would be about an hour before the authorities could show up. Laryn thanked them and hung up.

While they waited, Mrs. Anderson made fresh coffee. They didn't talk much as it seemed the lady was disoriented and shaking. Laryn watched her like a hawk in case she fainted.

In a vacant way, Mrs. Anderson said, "My daughter will be happy about the horse. I wonder if that was our old bull that was killed?"

Laryn shrugged.

They drank the coffee and that seemed to help them both.

ON AND OFF THE BEAT #12

Laryn was back in her car. She had called her brother on her cell phone. He was going to feed his players hamburgers in Winthrop. She told him not to wait for her. She was still waiting for the police to show up. She heard loud screams through the phone. His team had scored at that minute, so she didn't think he had heard what she said.

"Yeah, yeah!" was his answer as he hung up.

Laryn had answered all the questions the law had required and left her number to be reached at the Mount Vernon Police Station. She mused over what had happened as she drove back home. Another dead end and she did mean 'dead'. Recording the license number of the truck and asking permission from Mrs. Anderson, she checked the truck log book. It hadn't helped much in her research into the death of Maya. These things she didn't talk about to the local police.

Now what to do when she did get home? Laryn remembered a line her mother always used when she got stuck with writer's block A Laurel and Hardy sitcom. "It's another fine mess you've got us in, Stanley." Or was it Oly? It didn't matter as it was still a fine mess.

Okay, what did she know? Bubba might have given Denny's number out to girls, so he wouldn't get caught if he had a family. That made it seem plausible that Bubba had a family. He was still her most likely suspect. Did Maya have a local boyfriend? She hadn't checked that out because Maya was supposed to be on vacation with Bubba. Were there any clues left at the scene of the crime? Maybe she could talk to one of the detectives on the case.

Periodically her mind went back to the scene at Mrs. Anderson's. Mrs. Anderson had identified the body when they brought it out in a body bag from the barn. Laryn thought it was fortunate that she didn't get to see the stretched neck of the cadaver. It still swayed before her eyes in a bizarre way.

That leather skin stuck in her thoughts in a historical way. No wonder the Indians were able to make skin pouches and products from their enemies' bodies. Skin for drums being one of the commodities. She wondered how many other nationalities did the same thing over the course of centuries.

'Tan me hide when I'm dead, Fred,' from Australia came to mind. It was a thought, fascinatingly grotesque in nature that made her shiver. And now that little ditty wouldn't leave her mind as she drove on.

It was dark now and going over a pass on the North Cascades highway required enough concentration to null her mussing for now.

At home again, she called her brother. "How did the game go?"

Dayne answered gruffly, *"We lost, but it was a good game and now I can work on our mistakes. Quinn had a good time, but was worried about you."*

"I had a problem I was working on, but it didn't pan out the way I thought it would."

"How was that?"

Laryn grimaced, "I found a dead body at the house where this trucker I was investigating lived. I think it was the trucker."

"Good grief, Laryn. Do you find bodies everywhere you go?"

She snickered, "Just about and here I am, just a homebody at heart."

"Yeah sure, as you break somebody's knee cap."

"Hey, I'm not the gangster here. But I will keep it in mind the next time we play a game together."

"Okay, I'm warned. Now, I have to get some sleep. It's been a long day."

"That it has, dear brother. Good night."

She felt dirty. Taking a hot shower and using lots of girly soap, she felt like the sight of death no longer lingered in her mind or on her body. At this rate she wouldn't have any skin left if she found many more dead people.

Laryn retired for the night. Tomorrow was another day. Maybe something would turn up in the investigation. Maybe the sheriff's department would come up with some new information.

At her desk the next day, the dispatcher put a call through to her.

"Officer Scott, this is Lucy from the truck stop. I took Maya's place when she didn't show up for work."

Unseen, Laryn nodded. "Yes, I remember you. What's the problem?"

"I don't have a problem, but you asked if I knew a Bubba. I don't really know him, but I've kept my ears open since then and I have heard people call this guy Bubba. I took a phone picture of him, but didn't talk to him. He seemed like a nice guy."

Again, Laryn nodded. "Many people seem like nice people until you get to know them. My advice is to always be careful of people you meet for the first time. Anyway, I'd love to see the picture you have. When can I meet up with you?"

"I'm on duty right now. It was my break, so I thought I'd try to call you and if I didn't get to talk to you, I'd leave a message."

"I really appreciate your calling me. I'll be right out and see that picture you have."

"He won't be here. He left some time ago. I just didn't have time to call you until now."

"That's all right. I just wanted to ask him some questions about Maya." Laryn thought quickly. She didn't want to spook Lucy or Bubba. "Since he wasn't with Maya, he probably doesn't know where she went anyway."

"You could be right. He was flirting with the other waitress, but he still seemed nice."

"Thanks for calling, Lucy."

"You're welcome. Bye for now."

Before Laryn left for the café, she called the sheriff's department. When the dispatcher answered she asked for Detective Smith. Woman to woman might get the answers she wanted.

"I'm sorry. Detective Smith is out, but Detective Fenton is in today."

Laryn made a grimace, "Could I speak to him then?"

The gruff voice answered. *"Detective Fenton here. What can I do for you, Officer Scott?"*

"I've just got back from eastern Washington. Have they identified the body found out at Mr. Torenos' house?"

"Forensics says it was a woman. DNA hasn't come back yet. Mr. Toreno identified his daughter's suitcase from the clothes inside. We're assuming it was his daughter we found. I'm not telling you anything that won't be in the paper tomorrow. The reporters are tuned into our radios, so even being careful they're on us like fleas on a dog. Smith is trying for damage control out at Toreno's place."

Laryn rubbed her hand over her face. "Poor Mr. Toreno. Did you find any clues to what might have happened that you can share with me?"

"As you know, if we did, I couldn't tell you, but just between you and me, no, we didn't find anything. Forensics might have, but anything visible just wasn't there."

"Thank you, Detective Fenton. Maya was my friend and I feel bad that something might have happened to her. It also left Mr. Toreno with no one anymore. It is a sad case."

"Good talking to you, Scott," and he hung up.

Well, thought Laryn. He wasn't such a bad-ass man after all.

She straightened her desk and grabbed her jacket and hat. She skipped as she left the office humming. "I'm off-to-see-the-wizard, the wonderful wizard of Oz."

She gave Harve, on the desk, a salute as she left. "I'm going to check a lead at the truck stop."

Harve shook his head at her antics.

In Laryn's mind was the fact that she could have had Lucy just send the picture to her cell phone or e-mail account, but she didn't pass this information on to just anyone. She needed to know who had her numbers and who didn't. It was a pain-in-the-butt to change all her informational numbers if she was hacked.

Again she parked the patrol car towards the back of the parking lot. She picked a seat in Lucy's section in the restaurant. Lucy came over as quickly as she could, pouring coffee for patrons as she came.

"What can I get for you, Officer Scott?"

Laryn smiled at her, "The house salad and a roll will do and a cup of coffee while I wait."

Lucy smiled back while filling the coffee cup preset on the tables. "I'll bring it right back."

When Lucy came back, she had the salad and the roll, plus her cell phone tuned in to the picture Laryn wanted.

"I'll be back and refill your coffee for you."

She winked at Laryn and Laryn smiled back. Laryn looked at the picture. It was true the man was too old for the young Maya, but after you were twenty one, it was hard to tell ages or even care. Laryn sent the picture to her email at the office.

When Lucy came back, she sat down with Laryn. "I can take a short break," she said. "Did you send the picture to yourself?"

Laryn nodded, "I sent it to my office email. Did you see what truck he got in when he left?"

Lucy shook her head. "No, they are all parked in a tight row. You'd have to be staring at the fellows to see which truck they drive. None of us can just watch them without getting into trouble."

"I can understand that. I'd complain if I saw my waitress just standing there looking out the window and I wanted my coffee refilled. Can you tell me anything about him?" Laryn asked her.

"Not really. He wasn't at my table. He was at the counter and I have to pass by to get to the coffee. That's when I heard Trudy call him Bubba. I will say all the men flirt with the waitresses unless they're in a hurry or too tired to want to talk."

"So he seemed nice to you when you heard him flirting. He didn't seem over aggressive?"

"No, he just told Trudy she was pretty and she must have fellows falling all over themselves to date her. Trudy told him she was married and had the cutest little baby girl and would he like to see a picture of her. The guy even said yes he would. I didn't hear anymore as I had to fill cups again."

"Okay, girl, you did a good job. I thank you for keeping your ears and eyes open for me." Laryn left a good tip when she departed.

Laryn was cruising back to the station when a call came in on the radio for anyone in the vicinity of a life care center near by. Since Laryn was close, she took the call and responded with her siren going and lights flashing.

She pulled up to a lovely older lady waving her arms. She had a walker and nearby a wheelchair had tipped over. A kid with a cell phone was standing over the person on the ground.

He looked at Laryn and hollered, "The ambulance is coming."

The older lady was ringing her hands. "It's my son. We were out for a walk and some fresh air when he collapsed. The wheelchair was still going forward and veered off and fell over. I couldn't help him."

Laryn rushed over to the fellow on the ground. He wasn't a young fellow. She felt for a pulse. No pulse. Damn, she thought.

"I'll have to straighten him out so I can start C.P.R." She carefully turned him from his side to his back and started chest compressions for his heart to start. She could hear the ambulance coming.

His mother kept asking, "Is he all right? Is he all right?" She walked her walker over closer. "Dougie, wake up! Dougie, wake up for your mama!"

Dougie didn't stir and Laryn kept pumping. She didn't give him mouth to mouth as the new rule was that it wasn't necessary unless it was a drowning. The chest compressions were enough to get air into the lungs, but nothing would help the heart unless it wanted to be helped.

The paramedics arrived. They took over from Laryn. They worked on him for a short while. Dougie's mother was still trying to get him to wake up.

"He always was hard to wake up, but he always was a sweet boy. Dougie wake up!"

Laryn was crouched down by one of the medics. "That's his mother," she told the one closest to her.

The medics finally gave up. One of them took the lady gently by the arm. "I'm sorry, ma'am. He's not responding to us. There is no pulse. We're going to have to take him to the hospital. Do you have anyone who could take you there?"

She shook her head, "I drove over to see him today. He has Down's syndrome, so I try to see him once a week. I don't think I could drive right now. I'm pretty shook up about this. Did I do something wrong?"

The medic said, "No, ma'am you didn't. We'll need to get some information from you. We can do it here or up at the hospital if you can follow us."

The lady looked around confused. The kid who called 911 shrugged his shoulders.

Laryn spoke up. "I can take her up there. I'll just have to call it in, which I have to do anyway and I'll just add the hospital to my check-in."

The medic nodded and proceeded to put the patient on the gurney to wheel him to the back of the ambulance. The other medic took some information from the elderly woman.

"What will I do with his wheelchair?"

The young fellow said, "I'll take it back to the care center if you want me to?"

Even in her stress, the older lady smile and thanked the young man for all he'd done. Laryn walked the lady over to her cruiser and helped her in the front seat, folded her walker and put it in the back seat.

The ambulance took off with Laryn following. She felt like she was in a funeral procession as they didn't drive fast, just slow and steady. The only high-light was looking in her rear view mirror which showed the young fellow riding in the wheelchair racing towards the care center. A wheelchair Andretti, race car driver.

Laryn did her check-in and told Harve she could be reached at the hospital. The lovely older lady said, "We didn't introduce ourselves. My name is Gertrude Small. Dougie is my second son. Even though it was hard for him, he was always a sweet boy. He was even able to care for himself until just recently. I had to put him in the care center when he no longer could cook for himself and sometimes forgot who we were."

Laryn nodded, "I'm sure that was hard for you."

Gertrude smiled at Laryn. "I sometimes checked him out and took him to view the sound over by Anacortes. We just sat in the car and looked at the water and the seagulls flying around. He seemed to enjoy that."

They were at the hospital. Laryn came around and retrieved the walker out of the patrol car and then helped Gertrude out of the vehicle. Laryn followed her as she quickly went through the automatic doors and up to the receptionist. A nurse came to take them back to the room where Dougie's body was waiting.

"I'm sorry Mrs. Small, your son did not respond to our treatment. We're waiting for the coroner to release the body. You may hold his hand if you'd like."

Gertrude pushed her walker over to her son. She held his hand and talked quietly to him. She gave him a kiss just as the coroner came into the room. He gently asked her to leave as he checked out her son condition.

She and Laryn went back to the receptionist to fill out the necessary papers. The coroner came back out and asked her where she would like her son to be taken. She had the information, but not the papers for their family's burial preferences.

She looked at Laryn. "After I go kiss Dougie good-bye, could you take me home to my Independent Living facility?"

Laryn nodded, thinking it was so strange to have and older lady who was the mother in Independent Living with a son that was in a Life Care center. You never knew what life was going to throw at you.

Gertrude quickly came back. "I have to call so many people and make arrangements. I'll call my oldest son first as he can help me make decisions."

Laryn said, "Good idea." She helped Gertrude into the patrol car with the walker in back again.

As she dropped the elderly lady off, Laryn told her, "Now, you call me if you need any help: anytime, anywhere." She gave Gertrude her cell phone number.

"You are such a good girl, Officer Scott."

Laryn smiled to herself as she left. Good girl, huh. She no longer felt like a girl. She'd seen an awful lot of death just in a few months. It was a blessing she wasn't traumatized by it all.

She went back to the station to change her uniform pants. The knees were dirty where she had been on the ground giving Dougie C.P.R. Now she knew how the E.M.T.s' felt when they lost someone they were trying to save. It felt shitty, just plain shitty.

ON AND OFF THE BEAT #13

It was two days later when Laryn got the call at home from Gertrude.

"Ms. Scott, I have so much to tell you."

"Good to hear from you, too, Mrs. Small. What can I do for you?"

"Oh, I didn't call you for help. I just felt you needed to know what happened to Dougie."

This was strange. She knew what had happened to Dougie. Laryn asked in an apprehensive tone, "Okay, what happened to Dougie that I don't know about already?"

There was a giggle on the line. Strange for an older lady to giggle, let alone when her son had just died, thought Laryn.

"Well, shortly after you left me at home, I made calls to all my friends and relatives, then made arrangements for the burial. When my oldest son came to help me, and then I hung up. The hospital had been trying to reach me and couldn't get through. It seemed that jostling Dougie around had brought him out of his coma. My oldest son and I rushed back to the hospital. Dougie still didn't know us. But he seemed calmer when we spoke to him. I'm sure he recognized our voices."

Laryn was stunned. "You're telling me Dougie isn't dead? He came back to life?"

The voice on the phone was ecstatic. *"Yes, dear, that's what I'm saying. I had to call everyone back and cancel the funeral arrangements, but he is alive."* She quieted her voice down. *"I'm told not to get my hopes up that he will ever get to go home. They don't know what happened that he had no pulse and no heart beat, but maybe was breathing in a very shallow way. They more or less said many people must have been praying for him."*

"Mrs. Small, I don't know what to say. I guess I wish you well as we don't know what the future hold for Dougie."

Gertrude answered, a peacefulness to her voice. *"It has given me time to come to terms with his eventual death. I get to kiss him good-bye. That's a blessing in itself. When he goes, it will be time for him to go. His life was a good one even with his Down's Syndrome. People loved him and he loved people."*

Laryn was astounded. This lady had such inner strength and wisdom.

Gertrude made to hang up. *"I just wanted you to know. When you see his obituary in the paper, just say a small prayer for him and thank you for all your help that fateful day."*

"You are quite a lady, Mrs. Small. I'll always remember this day. Take care."

They hung up.

The next day when Laryn came into the precinct, she was all smiles.

Harve on the desk remarked. "What's got you all smiling at a place where mayhem reigns eternal?"

"You know that call that came out for someone to cover a person who fell over in his wheelchair?"

"Yeah," said Harve shaking his head and thinking, *'So what?'*

"Well, he was pronounced dead at the scene, but his mother called me today and said he had come back to life at the hospital when the coroner jostled him around. For a change I didn't find a dead body. This is a new day for me."

She raised her hands above her head and waved them back and forth as she danced back to the conference room. Harve shook his head at her antics. She did make working here a little brighter than it really was in a day.

Sunday was Laryn day off to go to her family home for dinner. She hoped Quinn Madden was there with her brother. She could use a good view of a superb body and if they hit a few baskets, maybe a sweaty, rippling muscular, body.

It had been awhile since she had been to the gym to work out. She'd even had to do some of her runs late at night. She hated that as invariably, she'd see something she didn't want to see and have to call it in and stay for the paper work involved.

Going in the house her mother met her and gave her an extra hard hug.

"It feels like months since we saw you. How have you been?" Her mother handed her a bunch of plates to put on the table.

"Fine, Mom. Who's coming to dinner?"

"Oh, just Dayne and his friend, Quinn. We haven't seen Quinn in quite awhile either."

Laryn grinned at her mother, "You mean Quinn willing gave up one of your Sunday dinners?"

Her mother gave her an exasperated face. "No, he had a muscleman contest he had to go to." Not thinking of her words, she added, "I guess they oil up their bodies and flex their muscles for a trophy."

Laryn about dropped the last plate she was putting on the table. "Mom, don't put images in my mind. I'm a susceptible woman, you know."

Her mother turned to her, surprise in her eyes. She giggled. "I keep forgetting you are a young lady now. That would be an interesting sight to see and, also, put in one of my romance stories that I'm writing."

Laryn shook her head. "You are so bad, Mom."

"Hey, I might be old, but I'm not dead yet. Isn't that what most men say as they ogle the pretty girls?"

"I hardly know enough men to know what they say. I'm around them all day, but they don't make smart remarks around me. I suppose it's part of the sexual harassment rules that keeps us from becoming friends that can say whatever they want to around each other. Otherwise, all the other men I meet just want to shoot me."

Her mother eyes widened, then she turned towards the kitchen. "Don't let it bother you. There's plenty of time for you to get to know more men and their foibles."

Laryn washed her hands as she helped to cut up vegetables for the salad.

She put the salad and dressings on the table, just as a loud couple of men came in the front door. Jordan, Laryn's father got up from the couch where he was watching a ballgame and loudly greeted Dayne and Quinn.

"Just in time, fellows, I can smell the sweet and sour spare ribs cooking and that means they are about ready to be removed from the oven." Jordan beckoned them with a wide sweep of his arm towards the dining room and on into the kitchen.

Dayne greeted his sister with a one-armed hug around her neck, almost cutting off her breath, or was that because she stood there looking into Quinn's bright blue eyes?

Quinn stuck out his hand for a handshake. She took it and neatly swung it behind his back, holding him captive with his back pressed up against her body. Bad idea as his heat filtered into hers. If she took him to the floor, she could have her evil way with him with her family looking on. Another bad idea.

"Hi, handsome," she quipped in his ear and let loose of his arm.

"Hi, yourself, and what did I do to earn that show of police brutality?"

She grinned at him. "It was either that or back-kick my brother where he might not procreate anytime soon."

"Children, children, knock it off. Jordan, take the ribs to the table. Dayne, get a hot pad for the ribs, Quinn, grab this rice bowl," as she shoved it at him, "and, Laryn, here are the hot rolls."

Obediently, the kitchen crew did as they were told. Eventually they all took their seats at the table. Grace was said and the passing of food or plates followed. Laryn thought it was interesting to note that they all took the same seats as they had in the past. Evidently, Quinn was now part of the family and had his seat assignment established.

When the first pangs of hunger had been quelled, Dayne looked at Laryn, "Found any new dead people lately?"

Samantha was horrified. "Dayne, we do not talk about dead people at the dining room table and especially when we are eating."

Laryn spoke up, "I don't mind this time, Mom."

She turned and looked at Dayne. "Yes, I did, but it turned out I may have contributed to saving his life."

"Do tell," countered her father, a quizzical look on his face.

Laryn abandoned eating and excitedly told her story. "I got a call to an emergency up near the Life Care Center. A fellow had overturned in his wheelchair. It turned out his mother, in her walker, had taken him out for a stroll. He lost unconsciousness and his chair kept going and overturned." Laryn looked the table over to see if they wanted anymore of her story.

They were all looking at her. "I gave him C.P.R. until the medics showed up. He didn't have a pulse and showed every sign of having died, but they worked on him before they shook their heads and loaded him into the ambulance. I took the little old lady up to the hospital where she kissed him goodbye and I drove her back to the Independent Living complex where she lived."

Laryn nodded to the people at the table. "She was about ninety years old and her son was in his sixties. Well, she called all her relatives, friends and arranged his funeral. She called me about two days later and in an excited voice told me he wasn't dead, that in jostling him around, he woke up. He's not really all there, but she said she gets to say goodbye to him and that was a blessing to her. She's a really neat lady."

Quinn was the first to speak. "That's amazing. You must be proud of yourself in helping to save a life."

Laryn blushed, "Yes, I am and I needed that. I've found too many bodies lately and it was beginning to get to me." In her mind, the dead eyes of those bodies stared at her kind of white and sightless. She shivered.

They all started to eat again and each, in their own way, were clearly contemplating this event and trying to imagine what had happened.

Dayne was the first one to shake his head. "Okay, what do you think happened to the fellow?" He threw it out to those at the table.

Jordan looked at Laryn. "Did a doctor see the fellow?"

She nodded, "Yes, the doctor, the E.M.T.'s, the coroner and myself thought he was dead."

Samantha smiled, "It's called the Lazarus Syndrome. When Christ told Lazarus to rise up from the dead and he did. You know I do a lot of research for my books and one western that I wrote had me writing a scene about a graveyard where they buried people in a casket with a string tied to the dead person's hand that was attached to a bell above the grave. After the person was buried, the gravedigger sat there for three days to make sure they hadn't buried someone alive."

"Oh, Mom! Ugh! And you tell us not to tell gruesome stories at the table." Laryn was appalled. This was not Sunday dinner conversation unless her mother instigated it and apparently she did just that.

Not intimidated, Samantha went on. "It seems like once in a while they had to dig up some caskets when a family wanted to move it to their own cemetery and found fingernail scratches inside. Some of this information went clear back to the dark ages where it was thought to be a form of torture."

Jordan had had enough of this talk. "What's for dessert, Sam, or should I tell you all stories I know about the fellows who lose fingers with the saw in cabinet building?"

There was a general shaking of heads and murmured "No's" at the table.

Samantha told them all to grab something off the table and clear up the remains of the Sunday dinner.

The word, *remains*, had Dayne grabbing his mouth in a gag motion. Evidently, when Samantha was on a roll, they all had to suffer.

ON AND OFF THE BEAT #14

Laryn did her run the next morning and day-dreamed about Quinn and his sweaty body when he had taken his shirt off. The basketball game had gone just fine until she kneed Dayne in the back of his knees and sent him to the ground. The cry-baby had scratched his knee and had gone into the house to get his mommy to fix it up.

She'd taken the blame, but it had ruined the game and they all went home. Her mother was upset that Laryn was turning into such a tomboy. Duh! She'd been a tomboy all her life, but now was supposed to turn into a girly-girl.

She guessed she should call some of her girlfriends and see if they wanted to do something. Unless there was a class reunion, she didn't see much of anyone anymore. Maybe she could get some tickets to a McIntyre Hall program and invite someone along. At that thought all she could think of was Quinn.

She finished her run with nothing decided except to shower and go to work.

When she got to work, Harve told her to call the detectives working on the Toreno case.

When she got to her desk area, she called the Sheriff's department. "Could I speak to either Detective Smith or Detective Fenton?"

"This is Detective Smith, how can I help you."

Oh, good, thought Laryn, she'd reached the woman detective. "This is Laryn Scott of the Mount Vernon police. You wanted me to call you?"

"Yes, we did. Mr. Toreno says you know more about this case than he does. We're investigating the boyfriend in the Toreno case. Mr. Toreno says the boyfriend isn't involved according to you."

Laryn felt confused for a second, "To which boyfriend are you referring?"

"*She had more than one?*" Detective Smith's voice rose in a demanding tone.

Oh, oh, thought Laryn, I stepped in the slippery stuff. "Maybe I should meet with you and go over all the details I have which are only speculations."

The detective answered back in a decisive voice. "*I'm disappointed in you if you have held anything back from us. You are a police officer and should know all information is vital to a case.*"

"Shall I come down there or do you want to meet me here at my desk?"

"*It depends on the information. Do you have a file on it?*"

"No. No file. As I have said, this is only speculation, not fact and not my case as it is out of the city limits."

"*I'll come to you.*" And the detective hung up, sounded as if she was in a snit about it.

Laryn dug her phone out of her shirt pocket and laid it on the desk. That was all the real evidence she had. The rest was just what she had done in her suspicion of what had gone down. And who was this boyfriend they were investigating? Laryn didn't know of another boyfriend, but she didn't know that much about the life Maya had lived. And what if that wasn't Maya they had found?

It wasn't long until Detective Smith and Detective Fenton arrived at her desk. Oh, oh, she thought. I guess I'm in trouble now and they've sent out both guns today.

Laryn stood up and indicated two chairs to sit in. They sat down, but did not crack a smile or shake hands. Laryn picked up her cell phone.

She looked at them. "This is really all I have and I've had to speculate on the rest."

Laryn played the recording. *Are you there, Laryn? Please pick up the phone. He's so mad he says he's going to kill me.* A pause in the recording. *Oh no! Please no!* screamed the voice. A scuffle followed by a thud, then the phone was hung up

Smith looked at Laryn, "That's all you have?"

Laryn nodded, "That's all I have and I proceeded from there."

Felton asked, "Who was that?"

"I didn't know and I had to think of all the friends I might have known with a slight accent. I could only think of two and I called to see which one it might be. Estelle Baronia's mother said she was on vacation for a week with her boyfriend. I left a message on Maya's house phone and asked her to call me back. Her father called me and said Maya was on vacation with a friend, too. I had to wait until Estelle called me back all happy and excited, but I had no call from Maya until Mr. Torreno became worried about her since he hadn't heard from her and felt she should have been back by then."

———

"You didn't know who this caller was then?" said Detective Smith.

"No I didn't. I did ask for the telephone records with Mr. Toreno's permission. I did find a call Maya made about the same day as she was to leave on her vacation. What did you detectives find?"

"We didn't ask for the records as we didn't know about the call until just recently when we approached Mr. Toreno about a boyfriend of hers, who is a neighbor," said Felton, in a deep accusing voice.

In a more feminine voice, Smith quickly said, "The boyfriend was very upset over her disappearance."

Laryn shook her head, "Well, I didn't know about this boyfriend, either."

Fenton again, "We're getting a little off the subject of why we came over here to interview you, Officer Scott. What did you find in the telephone records that might be of interest to the case?"

"I called the number in eastern Washington and the caller told me to never call again and hung up. In a reverse directory I found an address. When my brother had a game over there with his high school's second team, I went over to cheer him on. While I was there I called on the lady who lived at the address. She told me truckers often give out other trucker's numbers just to make trouble." Laryn looked at them sadly. "Her husband couldn't have taken Maya on a vacation as he was dead."

Detective Fenton seemed bound to make trouble for Laryn.

"Why didn't you tell us before now?"

Laryn raised her arms in surrender. "I was just looking into things for Mr. Toreno since his daughter was a friend of mine. I knew this wasn't my case and I'm the one who called you when we thought something was wrong. You might go to the truck stop and look into a fellow called 'Bubba.' I've been wanting to talk to the fellow, but if you go in there all gung-ho he might never stop there again." Now Laryn was getting a little hot under the collar. This was her friend and these detectives were more interested in her testimony than finding out things on their own.

Detective Fenton stood up. "You realize this is our case and we'll take it from here." He turned and stomped out.

Detective Smith shrugged, "He means well, but steps in where angels fear to tread. It's nice for backup, but in an investigation, I'm the one who has to keep the peace." She grinned, "Good cop! Bad cop! You know." and left the room.

Laryn stewed over the questioning from Fenton and Smith. How dare they think she had withheld information that they could have found out by a little detective work on their own.

She decided to call the coroner's office. Maybe they had identified the remains and would give out that information. The coroner's office answered.

Laryn said, "This is Officer Scott of the Mount Vernon police department. I was there when a body was found out at the Torreno residents. Have you identified the remains yet?"

A deep voice answered, *"Strange that you should ask at this moment. We just got the results in from the forensic lab. The person wasn't who we thought it might be. We don't know yet who this person was. It is a female, probably in her late teens or early twenties, dark hair, maybe of Latina descent, about one hundred twenty pounds. If you'll go through your missing person records, we might put a name on her. A report will be going to the different precincts soon."*

Laryn was stunned. It sounded like Maya, but they had Maya's suitcase so they should have her DNA. Just what was going on here? "Sure, sure, I'll do that and try for a match. Thank you for the information."

"We wouldn't have given it out to you, but since it wasn't who we thought it was, our next step is to contact the different departments of law and get out a description to try to identify the victim.".

"Thank you, sir, for the information. I'll get right on it and see what we can do."

They hung up.

Now where did that leave the case of the missing Maya, thought Laryn? She needed to talk to the other boyfriend, the neighbor. Mr. Torreno would be at work right now. Maybe this evening she would contact him and maybe talk to the boyfriend. Maybe he saw something the day Maya disappeared. She was just full of 'maybes.'

Elbows on the desk, her hands framing her jaws, she stared at the computer. It stared back at her and changed to a screen saver. Just then her desk phone rang. Ah, saved by the bell, thought Laryn. She picked up the receiver. "This is Officer Scott, how may I help you?"

"Oh, I'm so glad you're in. This is Lucy at the truck stop. Bubba is here. He just came in, so should be here for awhile."

"Thank you, Lucy. I'll be right there, only I'll change into my regular clothes so I won't scare him off."

They both hung up. Laryn rushed into the locker room and changed into jeans. Under her uniform shirt, she had a T-shirt. It was used for padding when the bullet-proof vest went on. At the front desk, she told Harve where she would be and why.

He asked her, "This is not your case, Laryn. Should you be doing this?"

"I'm afraid to miss this chance. I'll share what I know if I find out anything. Meanwhile, if necessary, I'll take a half-day leave of absence."

Harve nodded, "Works for me," he said.

Laryn took off in her own car. She luckily hadn't jogged to work today.

At the truck stop, she went in and sat in Lucy's section. Bubba was at the counter. She didn't need to talk to him, she just needed to get his truck license number. She had parked today where she could get the number when she saw which truck he got into.

Today was different. He was talking to another girl of Mexican descent. Since Laryn had come in late, she didn't know if the girl was with him or not. Lucy gave her a cup of coffee.

Laryn put five dollars down on the table. "I'll not eat today, so I can leave when he does." She cranked her head towards Bubba. Lucy nodded and left her alone.

Laryn looked around the room and noticed people eating. She looked out the window at all the trucks neatly parked in rows. How they got so close together was another mystery. Maybe the painted lines for parking helped them to just be able to get the doors open to get in the truck. She was a good driver, but had never parked a truck and trailer.

Ah! Bubba was getting up to leave. The young Mexican girl was leaving, too. Strange. She left the five dollar bill on the table and by-passed Bubba and the girl as he paid their tab. She got into her older model car and waited. Soon Bubba and the girl climbed into one of the trucks. It had been running, so must have a refrigeration unit in it.

Thank God, she had been trained to get license plate identification in a hurry. She also followed him out of the lot and wrote down other information she might need like container and trailer licenses, plus the name on the cab door. There seemed to be other licenses numbers for other states and the cargo company name. When he turned off to go to the main highway, she didn't follow him. She didn't need too, but it would have looked suspicious, also.

She rushed back to the precinct. It didn't matter now if Detectives Fenton and Smith did scare Bubba off, she had the information she needed to proceed with the investigation. Where it would lead was anybody's guess.

"That was quick," observed Harve.

Laryn nodded and rushed back to get into her uniform. This part was stupid, but she didn't want to be written up as being on the job and not being in her uniform. You could arrest someone when you were out of uniform, but when you were on duty or at the precinct you'd better be official.

At her desk, she jumped into research. DMV records showed a fellow named Earl Bubdecker owned a truck with that license plate. It was a cargo truck, so could pick up containers or loads of anything, usually on contract. His home address or business was in eastern Washington. Checking her notes was strange. Bubba's truck company was called 'Anywhere Trucking'

The reverse telephone directory had no phone listed. That made sense in this day and age as lots of people only used cell phones. If he had a family, they probably had the family plan that had multiple phones on it, plus he could just buy a disposable phone, too.

It would mean if Maya wanted to call him, she would have had to have a cell phone number. That meant he must have called her and she told him about calling the number he had given her and that was why he was so mad at her. All supposition, darn it.

The yellow pages in the phone book didn't have any information. Of course, the address for Earl Bubdecker was in eastern Washington and only a company name would be in the yellow pages of a telephone book, but again, no '*Anywhere Trucking*"

She had one other source she could tap. The truck scales on Bow Hill might give her some information on how trucking worked. She'd have to do this after working hours as it was out of her jurisdiction. She had her wallet and badge and would leave a message at Harve's desk that she might be checked out by the people at the truck scales. Good! She had a plan. Now let's hope no emergency came into the precinct before she got off duty.

ON AND OFF THE BEAT #15

The truck scales was up on a hill nestled among evergreen and deciduous trees and lit up like a city decked out at Christmas. You could see it reflected in the sky long before you got there. There was a state patrol car parked off to the side. Laryn decided she should check in with the patrolman before she tackled the men working inside the building.

The patrolman got out of the cruiser and walked toward her. "You got a problem, young lady?"

It was a question and not an accusation.

"No sir, I don't. I'd like to question one of the fellows in the weigh station on how trucking works." She paused, "I'm going to reach into my purse and pull out my I.D." Laryn was telling the officer this as these kinds of sudden moves put an officer on edge. She knew this from her own experiences.

He checked her credentials and said, "All right, I'll check with the fellows and see when you can question them." He went into the building and conferred with someone in there. He came out and talked to Laryn. "Ms. Scott, the fellows say to wait for a break in trucks coming in and then they'll talk to you.

She nodded and went back to sit in her car. It would be awhile, as there was quite a line-up.

After about an hour it seemed that the trucks entering the weigh station had stopped for now. One fellow from the building motioned Laryn to come forward. She had her identification out and ready to show him.

She held out her hand. "Hi! I'm Laryn Scott. I'm not on duty right now, so this is an informal request."

The fellow nodded. "Do you mind if I pour myself a cup of coffee?"

Laryn shook her head. "No, go ahead."

He looked back over his shoulder. "I'm sorry. Do you want a cup?"

Again she shook her head.

He came back to where she was standing. "Now, what can I do for you and call me Fess, like in the T.V. show, you know, Fess Parker?"

Laryn didn't know. This fellow was as old as her father. She'd ask her dad next time she saw him who Fess Parker was, but for now, she had questions to ask this Fess.

"I'm hoping you can answer some questions I have about how trucking works. It will help me in knowing when to stop a truck for an infraction, or when to leave it up to the State Patrol."

Fess nodded, "Ask away, Ms. Scott."

"How do you know which truck is stopping?"

"Good question. We have what you call a transponder. It triggers a truck's statistics: the name of the company, the driver, what it carries, its weight, length. It gives us the speed it has been going and the time between stops. If everything is okay, he gets a green light to go on. The trucker can get a fine for getting here too soon or even too late without a reason. If it is overloaded, over width or length, it has to stop and we check to see if the proper papers have been obtained."

Laryn was amazed. "So it is more than just being a driver. You need to be on your toes and alert to everything your truck is doing or where it is going."

"That's right, you do." Fess was impressed. He didn't have to go over the finer details. The lady cop got it on the first go-around.

"Do you keep a list of these drivers with an address and driver's license?"

He nodded, "It goes into the computer. The owner can track the truck, its load and contact the driver if needed. We don't have to do much of that anymore due to the magic machine and cyber space." He raised his eyebrows and looked at the sky as he chuckled. Then he looked serious again. "Oh, one thing I didn't tell you is that private owners of logging trucks do not have to stop here. They may need the same permits for over-loads, widths and so on, but the State Patrol stops them for that, and to check their permits and sometimes escorts them through a problem area."

"Where do these independent truckers get their information about loads for their truck?"

"There is what is called a Freight Broker. You have something you want delivered, you call the Freight Broker and they post it. The trucker checks to see what load he can get and where it is going. He also can get the information on a load to bring back, so no time is wasted just driving an expensive truck around."

Laryn had one more question. "How easy is it to go between Canada and the U.S.?"

"Not bad if your papers are in order. It just takes a passport or an enhanced driver's license. It's harder to get back into the states than it is to go into Canada. It depends a lot on whether you have a load going into Canada or bringing a load into the states. If you're honest, you usually don't have any trouble. You may be checked or searched, but they do that to cars as well." Fess looked beyond her.. "Oh, oh, we have customers coming. Good to talk to you Ms. Scott." He finished his coffee quickly.

"Thanks, Fess. You've been a great help. I'll be a better officer after this interview." She saluted him and left to talk to the State Patrol officer.

The officer was leaning against his patrol car. "How did it go?"

Laryn was all smiles. "It went great. Fess was very forthcoming about the job they do. I'll be able to analyze the trucks that go through Mount Vernon to know if I need to stop them for an infraction or not. Thanks for your help." She shook hands with him and left.

When Laryn got back to her apartment it was too dark to enjoy the river view. She poured herself a glass of white wine in her girly glass with the dangling earrings. She needed someone to talk to. From habit, she turned on the evening news and sat down on her couch. With the glass balanced on the couch's arm, she talked to it.

"Okay, what I heard is if you belong to a company, they track you through cyber space. If you own your own rig or logging truck, you are on your own except for any permit you might need. Is that right?" Laryn stared at her girly glass. It wobbled some, but finally nodded its head.

On the news were more shootings in Seattle. She pondered that information. Man, those cops took their life in their hands every time they went out. Back to her own problem.

She looked her glass in its questioning painted blue eyes. Its smiley face had kissy lips ready to speak to her if needed. She then took a sip. "I can't track Bubba through the cyber space. He could be trucking from eastern Washington on SR20, down SR9 from north of Sedro-Woolley or even on Interstate 5. All I really know is that all roads lead to Mount Vernon." Her glass didn't hesitate in nodding 'yes' by swinging the earrings back and forth. Even the necklace around the stem bounced.

The news said there were grass fires in eastern Washington and wild fires in California. Many firefighters were being deployed. Her eyes were on the T.V. screen, as her mind noted it, but inwardly she was focused on her problem.

Suddenly, she put her glass up in front of her face. "You're right. I need to stop the truck and get the information I need. Look out, Bubba. I'm on your trail." She drank the last dredges of her wine.

"Thanks, girly, for sorting my thoughts." She looked quizzically at the glass. She may need to name her. It was too smart to just be called 'girly.' 'Calli' might work, from one of the Crime Scene Investiation shows.

Laryn turned off the T.V., put Calli on the counter, checked the locks and went to bed. Another day, another dollar.

It was her day off. Instead of running, she decided to go to the gym. She'd check to see what Quinn was doing. If nothing else, it would get her heart rate up without too much exertion of energy.

She felt like being lazy today, followed by a cholesterol-making big fat Hawaiian burger later. Maybe even sweet potato fries with a small salad on the side with oil and vinegar dressing, something healthy to ease her guilt.

She was about to leave her apartment when the phone rang.

It was Detective Smith. *"I called your precinct and they told me it was your day off. I felt the information about that body we found out at the Toreno place was too important to you to let it go for two days."*

Well, this was a surprise after the reception she had received in her office the last time they had spoken. She thought they would never contact her again. "I'm glad you called. What is the information you have for me? I'm still concerned for Mr. Toreno and Maya."

"Well, you may be interested to know that wasn't Maya we found."

Now Laryn felt she had to act surprised. She knew that small bit of information. "It wasn't? That makes my day, but doesn't answer the question of who was it and where is Maya?"

"We don't know the answer to those questions. Another strange thing was the girl died, not from being murdered, but from a diabetes attack. Evidently she needed her insulin or juice or whatever a diabetic needs before she goes into shock and dies."

Talk about 'shock.' Laryn was truly surprised at that bit of information. "Wow! That really is news. I wonder why she ended up under the bales of alfalfa."

Detective Smith sounded like she was biting a pencil. *"Now that's the mystery. We don't know, but we will continue our investigation. After all, Maya is still missing. We have a dead girl we know nothing about. Her DNA isn't in the system. I'm hoping we can work together on identifying her, but Maya is ours."*

Laryn heard the censorship in Smith's voice. The conversation was done. "Thank you for giving me this heads-up on the case. I really appreciate it. If I find out anything, I'll let you know."

They hung up.

Laryn stood by her phone in a complete daze. Why would anyone put a dead girl under a pile of alfalfa when she had just died of a diabetic attack?

That could happen to anyone A hospital would have been a better place to take her. You could plead innocent of what was wrong and maybe even save her life. Maybe that neighbor boyfriend of Maya's knew more than he was telling Mr. Toreno.

Laryn grabbed her car keys. She needed to get to the Health Club. She needed to be on a machine and exercising in a mindless manner. Her brain could sift the facts more easily when she worked her body.

A quick thought when thinking of the Health Club. If she ever had Quinn in her life while exercising her body sexually with him, would she be solving cases during her throngs of ecstasy? "Jeez, Laryn, get real," she murmured as she drove to the club.

Naturally, the minute she hit the door, Quinn appeared from his office. Did he have a surveillance camera outside to alert him? Her face turned red just thinking about her thoughts driving here. Just looking at him drove her blood pressure up and heart rate to double time. Deep breaths, Laryn! Deep breaths.

"Hello, Quinn. I've come to work my body and brain. I just received some information I need to think about and I think better when I'm running or exercising. I didn't want to run today, so I thought I'd come over here and work out." Jeez, Laryn shut up. Your brain is leaking out of your mouth.

"And hello to you, too, my lovely Laryn. We'll get you set up on a machine and I'll leave you to your contemplating your problem."

She looked at him suspiciously. "Do you call every woman lovely?"

Quinn looked surprised. "Did I call you *lovely*?"

"Yeah, you did."

He grinned, "Well, maybe I meant my sweet Laryn."

"Ha, ha! You must have meant my snarly Laryn."

He laughed. "You always make my day, Laryn. Okay, hello, my snarly Laryn. Get your butt over here and get on a machine, so I can get back to my ugly paperwork."

Laryn laughed, "Now you're talking my language."

With his hands on her back, Quinn guided Laryn over to a rowing machine. "Gentle, easy motions while you work. None of that frenzy workout you usually participate in. Your mind will work in a comforting and informative manner that way."

If he knew how her mind was working, he'd run, not walk back to his hidey-hole filled with paperwork. She was sure his hand was imprinted on her back in a bright red, magic marker, outline. She watched him walk away with that tight rear end and broad shoulders beckoning her to follow him.

Why didn't she get turned on up at her folks' place when they all had dinner together? He had clothes on was one good reason. Even there he had the ability to look at her with those blue eyes of his that looked deep into your soul AND with a second thought; they usually were laughing at her.

That brought her back to rowing and thinking. Dead body not Maya—*Row, row, row your boat gently down the stream,*—Dead body not Maya—*merrily, merrily, merrily, merrily life is but a dream.* Repeat—repeat. It wasn't working. Her mind had gone blank. She might as well go eat that hamburger.

She got off the machine and walked back to his office. Leaning in his door, she said, "I can't concentrate. I'm going out and get me a big juicy, deluxe Hawaiian or Teriyaki burger and with each bite, let all the juice run down my chin and mop it up with sweet potato fries."

Quinn was startled at her leaning into his office. He had been concentrating on a bill and hadn't heard her approach. He smiled. It made his day to have her just acknowledge him. "You'll be sorry," he said in a sing-song manner.

She sing-songed him right back, "I know I will but I'll be a happy camper. Ta, ta." She waved her finger at him as she turned and left.

ON AND OFF THE BEAT #16

In the break room, Laryn encountered Farley Brunnell and Bay Renaldo. They all nodded at each other.

Laryn asked them, "Do you ever have to stop any of those trucks out at the Truck Stop?"

Farley answered, "Only if they have a light problem. I've stopped a couple over the years with burned out back lights. I didn't even give them a ticket. If they get stopped again, I'd nail them for an infraction."

Bay growled, "I'd have probably nailed them for something. I don't like to waste my time."

Laryn laughed and then wished she hadn't.

Bay snarled at her. "What's so funny?" His jowls bounced when he said *funny*.

"I was remembering us chasing that car full of kids on that drive-by shooting. We sure didn't waste time on that one."

Bay guffawed, "That was a fun ride, right?"

Laryn wished she could have covered her ears. His laugh nearly broke eardrums.

She nodded. "That it was. I wonder if the driver ever got his arm to working again. I really smashed it as I ran by."

"Served the bastard right. We don't like those kind of things happening on our watch."

Looking at both fellows, Laryn asked, "Do you think I'd get in trouble if I stopped a couple of trucks to see if their papers are in order? On my off time, I checked up at the weigh station and the fellow up there gave me a lot of tips on trucking. I need to get some information on a trucker and where he is taking his load. He usually takes some girl with him and the girls say they are just getting a free ride for a vacation. I don't even think sex is involved and we have this unidentified girl who died of insulin shock. Is there a connection?"

Farley didn't seem interested in the problem. But Bay's ears perked right up. "Let's ask the powers-that-be if we can do a truck shake-down. It should be fun."

'Oh God, oh God, did I let loose a monster cop?' thought Laryn.

Bay and Laryn checked with the sergeant on duty. With the small bit of information on what might have happened to the open case of the dead girl, the sergeant gave them permission to do a one-time routine check of the trucks. He even had a form for such checks.

"Now, I don't want any harassment of these drivers. We need to stay friendly with them and, also, not drive them away from the café where they eat. Play it cool, you guys. This is just a routine stop remember."

Both Bay and Laryn nodded. The sergeant could keep Bay under control it seemed. They collected their clipboards and left the room.

Back in the break room, Laryn cautioned Bay. "I need to get a hold of my informant and see if the fellow is over there today. It won't work for a one-time thing if the driver isn't there."

Bay looked surprised. "So you have someone specific you want to check up on?"

Laryn was skeptical of telling Bay all she knew, but she did need help. "My friend Maya was last seen with a trucker called Bubba. I'd like to know where Bubba goes on a routine trip. It wouldn't hurt to know where they all go, but that's asking too much and infringing on their privacy."

"Okay, but if it's not today, you may have to cross me off you list to help. You know I have duties assigned to me."

"Of course I know. So do I and those kids up at the school would miss my daily trip to check on them. They'd probably smoke marijuana that day and die." Her sarcasm was showing, but she doubted Bay would recognize it.

Bay scratched his head and looked hopeful. "Ya think they will?"

Laryn rolled her eyes at him. "Let me make my call."

The café answered. "Is Lucy on duty today?"

"No, she's not."

"Well, is Trudy on duty today?"

"Yes, she is."

"Could I talk to her?" Jeez, thought Layn, this is like pulling teeth and where did that old saying come from?"

Trudy came on the phone. *"This is Trudy, how may I help you?"*

Evidentially the guy on the phone must have shrugged when asked who was on the phone. "This is Officer Scott. I usually talk to Lucy, but she says you know who the trucker is, called Bubba."

"Yeah, I do. What's it to you?"

Laryn could hear gum snapping. "I was wondering if he comes in everyday or is he there now?"

"Why?" No gum snapping now.

"I am a friend of Maya's and he was supposed to take her to California on vacation. I just wondered if they'd come back yet. Maya hasn't called me, yet."

"I know Maya. She left us in quite a lurch when she didn't come back to work. Bubba usually comes in on Tuesday, about every two weeks. He didn't come in this week so maybe next Tuesday. I'll let you know."

"That's all right. I'll talk to Lucy when she comes back. Tell her I called, but don't tell Bubba about me as he might think he's in trouble and all I want to do is talk to him; friend to friend about Maya."

"I'll tell her. Gotta go." Trudy hung up.

Now, all Laryn had to do was her regular patrol and wait a week until Bubba might or might not show up. That was all right with her. It would give her time to come up with some questions that might help the case, but wouldn't alert the suspect, Bubba.

Quinn called Laryn about nine thirty that night. Laryn felt like a teenager talking to her boyfriend. She took the phone with her as she sprawled onto her couch.

Quinn was talking, *"I'll get right to the point. Would you and your family like to go up to the casino and watch the Chippendale's show? I know one of the guys. He used to do some of our muscleman contest shows with me."*

Laryn sat straight up, "The Chippendales?"

"Yeah, you know, like a strip-tease show only more sophisticated."

"Quinn, I know who the Chippendales are. I'd love to go, but I need to know when this is to take place and talk to my folks about them going. I can't see Dayne going unless women are involved, my dad is a maybe and my mother is not a prude, but do old ladies go to these things and with their daughters?" She emphasized the word *daughters*.

Quinn laughed. *"Your mother is defiantly not a prude and I need to pay her back for the many meals I get up there even if I'm Dayne's guest."*

Now Laryn laughed. "You think a few gyrating male bodies will be payback, huh?"

Quinn sounded dejected. *"I thought this might be something the family didn't get to do every day and they could meet my friend up close and personal. Maybe your mother would like to gamble while I take you to meet my friend and enjoy the show."*

"I shouldn't have teased you, Quinn. That was a very nice thought and I'll ask my family about a night out. Now, when did you say this was to take place?"

"It's short notice. It's this Saturday, but there are two shows, so we could go to the late one if your schedule isn't nine to five like a real human."

Laryn laid back down on her couch, propped up by a pillow and her feet on the arm rest. Ah, the better to enjoy the repartee of a potential date.

"I get off at six o'clock on Saturday. I have an early shift on Sunday, but Mom usually compensates that with a later dinner unless I can't be there at all. She says on Sunday is her contribution to the family and our catch-up time to find out what is going on in our lives. I appreciate it, too, as I find out what is going on in the family." She squirreled around on the couch. "There is this joke that if you don't keep in touch with your folks, they might move away and leave no forwarding address, because you don't care enough to keep in touch."

Quinn thought for minute, *"That would make you a twenty-something year orphan?"*

Laryn giggled, "I think Dayne would be in more trouble than I would. He lives at home and counts on Mom to fix him meals. I may not be my mother's cookbook, but I can feed myself."

Quinn smiled at her giggle in the background, *"I understand and I get most of my food at the co-op health food store. My meat is usually grilled. Those small red, green and yellow peppers skewered are great grilled with a little honey basted on them"*

"Quinn, you're making me hungry and after I ate the stew and biscuits Mom sent home with me, I felt too full to eat dessert."

"I agree those were good biscuits. Hey, I have to hang up. Please get back to me as soon as you can about the Chippendales. Even if they're sold out, I can get us in."

"I will. Good night. Talk to you soon."

They hung up.

Gosh, that was fun, thought Laryn. Just like the old days when she was in high school and had a life. Sometimes life sucked as an adult. You had priorities. Graduate from college, to getting a job, then create a new life style. She had done it all, but 'get a new life style.' She seemed to be in limbo. There was her exercising routine, her job, the after work stuff and Sunday dinner at her folk's place, but no life style, except dull, dull, dull.

It was late. Her mother often worked late at night on her writing. No one disturbed her at this hour. Laryn called her mother's cell phone. If she didn't want to be disturbed it would go to voice mail.

Samantha answered.

"Mom, this is Laryn. I'm sorry to disturb you. I thought it would go to voice mail."

"I forgot to turn it off." Distractedly, Samantha continued, *"What do you need, Laryn, as you must need something to be calling me at this time of night?"*

"Quinn wants to know if the family would like to go to the casino this Saturday and see the Chippendales. He has a friend in the program and would introduce him to us."

Her mother sounded excited. *"Laryn, I would love to go. I need some input for the book I'm writing. A sexy hunk would fit right in. I'm not sure I can get Jordan or Dayne to go. Carry your cell phone with you and I'll get back to you tomorrow. I have to go now while the muse is with me. Bye, sweetie."*

Laryn didn't get to say goodbye. Her mother was on a roll. She went to bed with her cat-clock rolling its eyes at her and wagging its tail, minute by minute. Did it know something she didn't?

The rest of the week went by without too much excitement. A stolen car was recovered minus gas in the tank, but no damage. A burglary turned out to be a cat that was knocking things over in a house when it wanted out because its owners had forgotten to let it roam before they went to bed. The scare was when the door was opened the cat ran out like an attack dog. Laryn, being on the bottom step of the porch, nearly got it in the face when it jumped off. Her quick reflexes saved her face from a nasty scratch.

Her date with Quinn and her mom and dad went off quite well if you discounted her mother. Quinn's friend was to die for. He was handsome, had sleek muscles, an oiled body and boy-oh-boy, could he dance. Laryn felt she could have had an orgasm just watching him. She wondered if her mother had, as she was the one whistling and yelling.

It was Sunday, so here she was at the house of her most embarrassing relative and Quinn was invited. Maybe he wouldn't show up. She went in the door. In the living room sat Dayne and her father.

Dayne looked up and pointed at her, and smirked. "I hear you enjoyed your night out with all those hot bodies."

Pointing to herself, "Me! Did Dad tell you about Mom's exhibition? That was the most embarrassing thing, AND, in front of Quinn."

Jordan laughed a good hardy laugh. "I'm sorry, Laryn, I should have warned you about your mother. While I was dating her, she drove me nuts with her antics. After I married her, she changed into this housewife woman I didn't know. I didn't kick her over into the ditch, because she still is the most beautiful woman I know, daughter excluded."

He wiggled his eyebrows at her, "I'm glad she hadn't changed as much as I thought." He gave her a thoughtful look, "Maybe we'll go to Karaoke one of these days. She can really rock the house and light my fire."

"Ugh!" Laryn threw up her hands, then looked at Dayne, "Did you know what kind of mother we have?"

Dayne just gave her that 'who me?' look and shrugged his shoulders.

The doorbell rang.

Laryn's face was like a deer caught in the headlight of a car. "Dayne, you go answer it. I don't know if I can look Quinn in the eye right now."

Dayne again shrugged his shoulders. "He's your date."

"Humph!" she snorted disgustedly as she stomped to the door.

When she opened it, Quinn pulled her out onto the porch and gave her a full arms hugging kiss. When he released her, she still had to hang on. She might be able to dodge a flying cat, but no way was she able to dodge a full blooded kiss and keep her equilibrium.

"What was that for?" she asked breathlessly.

Quinn grinned, "That's for you being such a good sport when we took your mother to the casino. I could tell, you wanted to sink into the floor when she jumped up and gyrated around her seat whistling with both fingers in her mouth, "yelling take it off, take it all off."

Back on her steady feet again, Laryn looked chagrinned. "It was so embarrassing, Quinn."

"Just to you, sweetheart. Other ladies were displaying the same pleasures. You just didn't notice because she was your mother." He gave her a gentle pat on the back. "I'm used to the antics of the audience. I'll admit I get a little worked up when it's men whistling and stomping their feet at the muscleman competitions. I'm not performing for men or women. I'm performing for the judges."

"I'd ask how you can stand it, but I have the same problem when I have to pat down the girls or women at the station and they ask me if I'm enjoying the feel. I'd like to punch them or slap their face, but I'm the law enforcement officer." She took a small step backwards and put her hands on her hips. Her chin came forward and she reiterated, "I'm the law enforcement officer. I'm the law enforcement officer and I can handle this even when they spit on me, damn-it"

Quinn's eyes sparkled. She was a raving beauty when she was mad. However, he was here to eat Sunday dinner and the longer they stood on the front porch, the more likely her family would imagine things that weren't going to happen, today at least.

"God, you're beautiful when you're mad. Let's go inside and eat some of your mother's fabulous food."

Quinn thought she was beautiful? That took some of the starch out of her spine. She hooked her arm through his and opened the door to go in, pulling him slightly as they both couldn't fit in the opening at the same time.

"Quinn's here," she yelled through the house, "and he's hungry."

Her sedated mother leaned into the door to the kitchen. Her sugar-sweet voice saying, "Hi, Quinn, dinner will be on the table as soon as Laryn helps me put it there. Go get the other men and tell them to wash up."

Laryn dropped Quinn's arm and rolling her eyes at him, left to help her mother.

The delicious fried pork chops with homemade applesauce was consumed as Laryn sat there quietly steaming while her father, Jordan and brother, Dayne, teased Samantha about her exhibition at the casino.

"Did you really do that, Mom?" questioned Dayne.

Jordan nodded his head, "She sure did."

Samantha thought Quinn's friend was to die for and felt she would use him in her novel. Were his eyes blue or brown was her question? Did he have a girl friend or was he gay?

Laryn's, "Moooom!" went unnoticed.

The men were going to clean the kitchen, so Laryn excused herself and went home. Her excuse was to clean her fish bowl and put new water in her vase of ivy.

ON AND OFF THE BEAT #17

It was Tuesday and time to set up the sting operation. Bay didn't have anything on his docket, so he was going with her. They'd take two patrol cars and station one on each road to an entrance to the freeway. They decided that they would check at least four trucks or more if Laryn didn't get to Bubba in that span of time. Laryn would get back to Bay if she found Bubba, but if Bay found Bubba, he would contact her and she would come to him, do some of the questioning and then they would both leave.

It sounded casual enough to them so as not to alert the truckers as to any problems. There might not even be a problem, but Laryn still thought something was fishy about Bubba taking girls to Disneyland in California. It seemed to be Hispanic girls he was interested in. Why not one of the other waitresses; Shirley, Lucy or Trudy?

Mr. Toreno was the only person who had reported a girl missing. Would other Hispanic people report their daughter or sister missing, or would they be too frightened to report them feeling deportation might be ordered?

Good questions, but no answers, thought Laryn.

Laryn had to go through the ritual of getting a hold of Lucy. When Lucy finally answered, Laryn stated her case.

"Sure, I'll call you as soon as he comes in. You should have about an hour before he leaves."

Laryn relayed her information to Bay. It was all Bay could do to maintain his impatiences. It was one of the few times reports came in handy. Do reports until the call came in, or an emergency took over.

Officer Farley Brunell was handling the patrols today. Laryn was gaining more respect for her compadres as time went on. They were working well together when they had a common goal. She still felt she had to give more energy to maintain her status than the men had to, but what the heck, at this point, she still loved her job.

Finally the call came from Lucy. *"He's here,"* was all she said.

Bay, in his patrol car, took the first entrance to the freeway. She took the second. She kind of hoped Bubba took Bay's route, so she'd be free to question the sidekick. She'd like to see who Bubba had beside him today. Would it be another Latina girl?

She had checked the stats on three trucks before word must have gotten out and the truckers started working Bay's route. It wasn't that anyone was doing anything wrong, the trucker's just hated wasting time with, to them, useless questions.

Bay gave two tweaks to his radio. This was the signal Laryn had been waiting for.

She drove over to help Bay. He asked her to hold the end of a measuring tape, while he measured the longest pipe on the load. When Bay gave her the okay, she went around the truck to the window where a girl sat in the seat. The girl rolled down her window.

"Anything wrong, officer?"

Laryn shook her head. "No, this is just a routine check we have to do now and then. Where are you going on this fine day?"

The young Latina girl smiled a beautiful, white teeth smile. "I'm so excited. I'm going to Disneyland and then if everything works out, I get to go see my cousins in Mexico. I've got my passport and everything."

Laryn was surprised. She hadn't thought of Mexico. This would give her food for thought. "Disneyland sounds like fun." She smiled at the girl, "Do your cousins know you are coming?"

"No, I'll call them from California. I don't know quite what our schedule will be or how many loads we have to pick up or deliver. I'm just so happy to get a free ride down there and a ride back when the time comes."

Interesting, thought Laryn. "Where are you from?"

"I'm Maria Hernandez from Ferndale where we picked up this load of drainage pipes."

"Glad to meet you, Maria. Have a nice trip."

Bay sent Bubba and his truck on its way. They had another truck lined up, so checked it in order not to raise suspicion and waved another one on. Their check-point stakeout was over.

When they got back to the precinct, Sergeant Diller was sitting on Bay's deck. "How did it go?"

Bay, all business now, answered, "All the trucks checked out okay. Here are the checklists."

The sergeant accepted them.

Laryn stepped forward. "Serge, can I study the one from Earl Bubdecker of '*Anywhere Trucking.*' He's the one I'm looking into in the disappearance of my friend, Maya Toreno."

"Sure, just file it in the proper drawer when you're finished and if you find anything interesting about the Toreno' case, contact me first, will you?" He turned to Bay. "You can go relieve Officer Brunell. He has a report due right away and I let him off just for you guys."

Bay saluted the sergeant and smiling about getting out of more paperwork, took off before the sergeant changed his mind.

Laryn took the information to her desk to study and make notes. She would need to ponder this latest information on Mexico. It made more sense for Bubba to take Latina girls if he was going into Mexico. They would be eager to get a free ride however dangerous it might be. Bubba was a good-looking guy and seemed to be personable. It would be easy for a young girl to trust him.

Laryn laughed to herself. She wasn't much older than these girls, but she felt ancient looking at it from a responsible adult's perspective. Maybe this job did age you. Look at how she cringed at her mother's actions at the Chippendale show and now she was cringing again at the actions of a young girl accepting a ride to Disneyland and points farther south. Ugh! She was getting old!

While the case was hot on her mind, she checked the telephone directory to see if Maria Hernandez had a telephone number. Maria didn't, but there were several Hernandezes in the book. If no one reported a missing girl in two weeks, Laryn thought it would be prudent to call them and ask if they had a daughter named Maria and was she still in California. She could pretend she was a friend and wanted to talk with Maria. Okay, she had another plan to follow.

Her conscience bothered her about not reporting to the detectives assigned to the Toreno case, but what did she really know to report? A truck driver named Bubba took girls to California and maybe on to Mexico. It was all supposition to support Maya Toreno's disappearance.

She'd wait until she could confirm that maybe Maria Hernandez was missing. It sounded callus to want Maria to be missing, but what if Maya was alive and well in Mexico and just hadn't called home yet? Maybe she couldn't call home without her cell phone. Maybe if Maya had a cell phone it couldn't be charged in Mexico without the right connection.

Laryn started writing her questions down to ponder later. Right now her mind was spinning with ideas and questions. She smiled at her thoughts. Maya might be alive and living in Mexico.

She called Feliz Toreno. When Feliz answered, Laryn asked, "Mr. Toreno, do you have any relatives living in Mexico that Maya might want to have visited when she went to California?"

"Si, we have relatives there, but they live way down below Mexico City. She would have a hard time getting to our little village in the hills. Why do you ask?"

"Well, I just found out that one of the truckers does go to Mexico from time to time if he has a load to deliver. If Maya had a passport, she could have gone over the border with no trouble."

"Si, she had a passport. We've kept it up for both of us in case we wanted to go for a visit. We've never used it because we never had no money or time. My truck isn't so reliable to travel so far."

Laryn understood Feliz's problems, "Is there any chance you could contact your family and see if Maya had visited them?"

"Si, I can write to them. My Spanish writing isn't so good anymore, but I will write and see if my Maya has been there."

"Thanks, Mr. Toreno. It is one more lead I'm following for you and Maya. Bye for now."

"You are so kind. Adios."

Ah, another lead she could follow. Laryn wrote this information down on her paper. She made a file for her personal information on this case and put it in her desk. She got up and filed the truck checklist of Bubba's with the rest of them. It was time to go home. It had been a productive day for her anyway.

She had to expend some energy. What better way than to go to the Health Club and work it off, plus she could drool over hunky Quinn Madden. She decided to hit the punching bag for awhile. Light weight gloves helped to keep her knuckles from being scraped. She punched and ducked, lurched and shoved. Her imagination followed a real-live action-figure. Today it was the green Incredible Hulk telling her what to do. She imagined his slightly accented voice telling her to jab, duck, sway and punch back with a right cross to the chin. She blinked. It wasn't the Joker or Lex Luther. It was just a bag she hit.

"Awww, and who did you punch today?"

She didn't need to know who had come up behind her. She could smell his spicy shaving lotion with an overlay of clean male sweat. She turned and saw Quinn Madden at his best, half dressed in a basketball jersey with his muscles all bulging and rippling. His cutoff jeans had a few strings hanging and one side was more jagged then the other.

"Hi, good-lookin'. You been playing basketball again?"

"Nah, a little handball with a fellow who needed a partner. Besides, I asked you first. Who did you smack around today to get you on the bag?"

Laryn grinned at him. "I had the best day and just needed to expend some energy. My friend, Maya, might still be alive."

Quinn took her arm. "Let's go over and get a bottle of ice cold water and toast the occasion. I need to cool off and re-hydrate my body."

They walked over to the ice chest Quinn kept for the iced water for his guests. He opened a bottle for Laryn and then himself.

"Okay, what's this about your friend being alive?"

"We questioned a truck driver, and his passenger was a Latina girl from Ferndale. She said she had a free ride to Disneyland and Mexico and had her passport with her. It got me to thinking that maybe Maya had gone on to Mexico to visit her relatives. Mr. Toreno is going to write to his relatives and see if she stopped by, although it is in a village off the beaten path."

Quinn laughed. "Take a deep breath, Laryn. That was a lot to say in one breath and excited at that."

Laryn started to jog in place. "Well, it is exciting. It is the first sign of hope we've had for Maya since her disappearance."

Quinn cocked his head. "Did she take her passport? I know, in the past, you mentioned she left her suitcase and a cell phone was smashed, but nothing about a passport."

Laryn looked startled, "I forgot to ask Mr. Toreno if Maya's passport was gone. Thank you, Quinn. I must rush home and call him before he goes to bed."

"You can call him from here. Come into my office." He turned and headed for his office with Laryn following him like a trained poodle.

Quinn handed her his phone. "You won't need this recorded will you? I never thought about that."

"No. It really isn't my case. I'm doing this as a friend, but I will report anything I get that is relevant to the detectives on the case." Laryn was talking as she dialed.

When Feliz answered, Laryn asked, "This is Laryn Scott. Did Maya take her passport or is it still where you keep it?"

She turned to Quinn. "He says he will look."

In a few minutes, Feliz came back on the line. *"It is missing, so she must have taken it."* He sounded upbeat for the first time since Laryn had talked to him.

Laryn cautioned him. "Don't get your hopes up just yet. This just gives us another lead to follow. Tell me when you get a reply from your relatives in Mexico."

"Si, si, I will. I like it you care so much, Miz Scott."

She hung up with a thoughtful expression on her face, then looked at Quinn and brightened. "Now we wait."

Quinn squeezed her shoulder. "Come on, lovely lady. I'm off duty, so I'm willing to buy you an artery blocking meal. We have several Italian restaurants that could serve the purpose for both of us. Can you wait for me to shower and change clothes here?"

"Don't get too fancy. As you can see, I'm in my after work grubbies."

Quinn looked her up and down. She had tight jeans on that outlined her svelte figure. Her T-shirt had ladybugs all over it giving it an informal style and outlining her firm breasts. "What's not to like?" he quipped was he left for the shower room.

When he returned, she had retrieved her jean jacket and purse from the lockers. He escorted her out the back way to where he had transportation waiting. Laryn looked around. There was nothing but a motorcycle parked by a dumpster.

"You have a shortcut to walk to one of the joints?"

"Nah, I have an extra helmet. You get to ride behind me on my favorite girl. Come on and straddle Nelly."

He handed her a helmet he must have picked up as they went out the door. She put it on ready for her first ride with Quinn. She had ridden motorcycles before and had qualified for a motorcycle license to ride as a cycle cop. She hadn't gotten that job, but still kept her license up. It wasn't her favorite form of transportation since it rained so much in Washington State, but that might change when she hugged Quinn around his waist. After putting on the helmet, she climbed on behind Quinn. Now this was the life—a reason to hug a handsome man and get away with it.

ON AND OFF THE BEAT #18

Two weeks were up since she and Bay had checked out the truckers and Bubba was definitely taking Latina girls to Mexico. She needed to do some calling on the Hernandezes in Ferndale. Did anyone have a daughter named Maria missing? She started writing down questions to ask people when she called them.

Her thought process kept getting side-tracked by the happenings over the last two weeks. The outstanding one was the high speed chase culminating in a suicide by police action and then finding it connected with a murder.

Yuck! When she and Farley Brunell had encountered an SUV going way over the speed limit in a rural area they had done the chase scene. The SUV finally stopped and the young fellow ran into the woods. As they came upon him, he pulled out a gun.

Brunell and Laryn both dropped to their knees with guns drawn. The fellow shot at Laryn hitting her in the chest. Her shot went flying off into the tree. Brunell's shot hit the mark and to their horror the top of his head blew off. While they watched, blood and brains flew everywhere, splattering the Douglas fir tree trunk red with blood.

Laryn couldn't breathe with the breath knocked out of her She closed her eyes, hoping when she opened them, the sight wouldn't be what she had seen. Her breath came back, but she hurt all over. No deep breathing for her for awhile.

It had been up to Brunell to call it in. Laryn helped photograph the scene and helped with the cleanup after the coroner ordered the body parts to be picked up.

It had been their duty to pick up all the pieces of bone and brains. The trauma of the hit to her Kevlar vest and the scene was too much. Laryn had to go over to the bushes and vomit. She wouldn't be eating bloody meat for awhile until she could get the vision out of her system.

The fellow must have been a logger as his cork boots had been covered in blood. The sharp calks even had bits of meat along with dirt and leaves in them. They had just finished their job when a call about a homicide made them alter their course. They discovered a mutilated girl dead and shot with a gun. It looked like before or after she was shot, someone had kicked her in the head and stomped on her with spiked boots. Her face was mincemeat. Another sight she had to get out of her head.

They'd have to wait for ballistic tests and investigating interviews, but to Farley and Laryn this was a no-brainer: their dead guy did it.

The only bit of humor on reflection was Farley's comment. "A little bit over-kill don't you think?" She remembered gagging, but not her reply.

Farley had to go on routine administrative leave while the investigation was going on. She just had to heal her bruises.

With extreme effort and her shoulder hurting, she put the events out of her mind and called one of the numbers in Ferndale for the Hernandezes. On the third call, she found a family whose daughter had gone with a trucker to Disneyland. The daughter had called them from Disneyland, but they hadn't heard from her in a week.

"A week, you say. Will she be home soon? I'm so excited to hear about her trip to Disneyland. I know she was excited to go there." Laryn grimaced at her lie, but she did know that Maria had been excited about her trip.

The English of the Hernandez's was very good. *"She told us she would be back in two to three weeks. It would depend on the load that 'Anywhere Trucking' got to start the drive home."*

"Do you think the truck would come all the way back up here or would they drop off a load and pick up another?"

"Since I'm not familiar with trucking, I couldn't say for sure. I wasn't happy with her going off with this guy, but to try and tell my girl that just made her angry. She's over twenty-one as you know if you're her friend."

"I figured she was though I was older and in a different class. We met in sports." Laryn figured, in the smaller schools, everyone played sports of one kind or another.

The woman laughed, *"Yes, she certainly liked her games. Softball was her favorite."*

Laryn laughed with her. "Could you have her call me when she gets back from California? I'll give you my cell phone number. I don't think I gave it to Maria before she left."

Laryn gave the woman her number. She figured the mother would call her if her daughter was missing too long and if Maria came back, Maria would call out of curiosity. She had never given the lady her name. If Laryn's mother knew that she hadn't given her name out right away, Laryn would have been raked over the coals on her poor phone etiquette.

Laryn held her head with both hands. Okay, another wait. Should she or should she not contact the detectives on Maya's case? She still didn't have anything to report, but she sure would like to know if they had found out anything to go along with what she knew.

She was about to check to see if anything had come up, when a call came in about a warehouse fire and she was ordered to help with crowd control. The police were first on the scene in these situations making sure no one was in the way of the fire trucks.

Taking one of the patrol cars, she arrived on the scene and helped string yellow crime scene, tape up. This also helped to keep the crowd back.

It was not a hard job, but as an officer of the law, she was supposed to look the crowd over for suspicious characters besides keeping everyone back. It was strange how a crowd, without thought, could creep forward without knowing it. When told to stand back, they acted like they hadn't known they had moved, but usually complied.

This bunch of people was mostly the workers themselves. Just then the fire engines came, and with the precision of a dance troupe, had the hoses out and water spraying on the burning building. One of the firefighters was yelling at the crowd to count their fellow workers to see if everyone was out.

One lady screamed, "My daughter is in the break room. They wouldn't let me go to her."

The fireman came over to get the details. "Where is the break room?"

"It's in the back of the warehouse. Darla wouldn't understand the fire bell. She was working on a puzzle. I didn't have a babysitter today and she was sick so couldn't go to school."

The fireman took off running before the lady had finished talking. He started yelling instructions to fellow firefighters. The lady was standing there wringing her hands and putting them to her face in an agitated manner. Laryn felt sorry for her and worried about the child herself.

Soon the firefighter was leading a crying girl about twelve years old by the hand. Her mother ran to her and they were hugging and talking although Laryn couldn't hear what was said.

The firefighter came over to where Laryn stood. "Hi, Laryn. I thought that was you."

Laryn got a good look at the fellow. "Billy Butler, how good it is to see you."

She put out her hand to shake his. In his hurry, he ignored it.

"Call me after work and we'll have coffee and catch up. He reached inside his yellow fireman's suit and must have found a pocket, because he withdrew a card and handed to her, then left before she could answer his invitation.

She quickly stuffed it into a pocket and looked around to keep her crowd under control. Crap, there was a fellow grinning at the fire and with his hands in his pocket, pumping it. Yuck! Laryn had heard about perps like this. He may not have started the fire, but he was enjoying the excitement. She went over and with him protesting his innocence, pulled his wrists out of his pants and cuffed him. His pants became wet as she walked him over and shoved him into the police car. The car would have to be washed with carbolic acid, if she had her way, and her hands would take all the sanitizing lotion she could find and then some. Eeew!

When she got off work, she went home to shower and change her clothes. She had a date with her high school crush. Billy had been a muscular wrestler and she had drooled over him without him ever knowing she was alive.

She gave him a call. Someone answered. "This is Laryn Scott, is Billy Butler there?"

"Sure."

Laryn could hear yelling in the background and then Billy came on.

"Hello, this is Bill Butler. What can I do for you?"

"Billy, this is Laryn and you asked me to call you after work. It sounds like you're still on duty."

"I am." And he gave her instruction on how to find his station.

Well, this wasn't quite what she expected, but it would be nice to talk over old times no matter where they drank their coffee.

She didn't need his instructions to find his station. After all, it was her duty to know where most things were in her jurisdiction. She arrived at the station and parked out of the way of any fire truck needing to leave the station quickly. She went in a side door that looked like an entrance. This must be the break room. Someone was cooking. A few were playing cards.

They all looked at her like an alien had invaded their territory.

"Is Billy Butler around? He's expecting me."

The cook swaggered over. "I'll be glad to take Bill's place. What could I do for you and I'll guarantee it will be better than what Bill could do?" He snapped his suspenders and smiled a beguiling smile at her.

Her eyes twinkled at the posturing of the cook. "I just promised to drink a cup of coffee with him and catch up on old times."

One of the fellows got up from the table and went to a door and yelled "Bill, you're wanted by a beautiful female, but none of us can figure out why she'd want a butt-face like you over us." The guy did a salute to Laryn and went back to the table.

A second later, the door flew open and Billy came swaggering in. Did all the firemen swagger, thought Laryn? Nah, she'd seen them running during the fire at the warehouse.

"Hey, lovely lady. Come sit down and I'll get us a cup of coffee and reminisce a little."

He cupped his arm around her back and led her to a corner table away from the prying eyes and tuned in ears of the other fellows. His arm was strong around her. He still had muscles galore. She felt like swooning.

Bill came back, "I forgot to ask you if you wanted cream and sugar in your coffee?"

"No, black is fine unless you have a latté machine in here." She replied with a grin.

He scowled at her. "No respected firefighter would admit he liked a latté." He sat down across from her. "So how's it going? I see you're a police officer now."

"Yes, and until this last week, I've enjoyed it and felt needed." Her second thought was why had she brought up this last week? What a way to kill a relationship. "I had to attend a murder, and suicide by cop. I copped one in the Kevlar vest, but my partner did the take-out."

He looked concerned. "Bummer, but I'm glad you weren't seriously hurt. Was it someone we knew?"

Laryn shook her head. "No, but I had to pick up the bloody pieces the fellow left behind which led me to up-chuck in the bushes. Not one of my finer moments with one of the fellows looking on."

He scrunched his face and changed the subject. "How's your brother doing?"

"Dayne? He's one of the coaches up at the school."

"Yeah, I read about him and the team in the papers all the time, but that doesn't tell me how's he doing?" He grinned at her as he patted her hand that was on the table.

Ah, she'd never wash that hand again. "I've got an idea. My mother has Sunday dinners nearly every weekend. Why don't you come to dinner this Sunday as my treat and you can ask him yourself. He lives at home, but certainly does his share of the work there. It works for Mom, Dad and Dayne, too.

Bill's eyes lit up. "I am off-duty this Sunday. What time and where and I'll even change my shirt to white." He rubbed his hands together. "This will be fun."

Just then the bell rang, the sirens went off and everyone jumped up but the cook.

Bill looked at Laryn. "Gotta run, but leave me a note on the bulletin board right there." He pointed to a board overflowing with notes and stick pins.

All the men disappeared out a door and within seconds the fire trucks took off. Laryn left a note for Billy, saluted the cook and left the way she had come in.

ON AND OFF THE BEAT #19

The rest of her week went smoothly and she finished many of the reports that had been due. She still hurt when she took a deep breath from the bullet hitting her Kevlar vest. Her right arm was bruised and the color streaked up her neck. Laryn had not told her family of her brush with death. Those people would have a fine old tizzy about that. It was enough to tell them about the bloody cleanup mess. She periodically worked her arm in a loosening motion as she worked.

Sunday at last! She had called her mother to expect another guest. She had, also, asked her mother to not have rare beef, since her episode with picking up body parts. She just couldn't handle that yet and didn't want to embarrass herself in front of Billy. Her mother gagged at Laryn's outrageous description of her suicide-by-cop gig.

She dressed very girly with a pink, tight knit, turtle-neck top and a swinging flowered skirt. Her strap sandals would do. She curled the front of her boy-cut hair style. Swinging flowered earrings finished out her feminine look. Maybe Billy didn't know how she had looked in school, but she wanted him to have a new memory of her at her finest.

She left early to help her mother with the dinner. It had been awhile since they'd had lasagna, so her mother had made the casserole. Of course green salad and garlic bread went with that. Tiramisu made with an easy recipe her mother had wanted to try, was for dessert.

Billy would think they were of Italian descent with a dinner like this. But then Billy looked more like an Italian, than this bunch of gigantic, blond people, except for her petit mother.

The gang converged on the Scott home about two o'clock. Dayne and Quinn came bursting in and the decibel of noise increased. Shortly thereafter, the doorbell rang and Laryn had to beat her brother to the door in a hallway scuffle.

"Welcome to the family home, Billy."

"Something smells delicious. Italian, I hope." Billy hugged her in a 'good-to-see-you-squeeze' and preceded her into the living room.

Dayne turned around and saw their guest. "Billy Butler, as I live and breathe. How's life been treating you?"

"Great and yourself?"

"Fine and I'd like you to meet Quinn Madden, who helps with the team's fitness and dietary training."

Quinn stood up as they shook hands. The fellows sat down and proceeded to talk teams, games and old times. Her father wandered in and joined the discussion. Laryn felt totally out of it. Billy had hardly glanced at her and had headed straight for Dayne. Were Sundays just for 'men' talk or for family get-togethers? It was up for grabs right now. She headed for the kitchen and 'women's' work. Ugh!

Her mother looked at her. "So, tell me about our new guest."

With a dreamy look in her eyes, Laryn asked, "You remember in high school when I took tickets at the wrestling matches?"

Samantha nodded, but kept working.

"Well, Billy Butler was one of the wrestlers and a *hotty* to us under-aged girls, who were lowly freshman and sophomores. I've had a crush on him for years. Say the word **Billy Butler** and I'd swoon."

Samantha laughed, "And we have two muscular men in there now. You must be in heaven with all that testosterone floating around our living room right now."

Laryn smiled, "We'll have to see how the evening plays out. I've never been in the popular-girl category, as I was too tall for most of the boys until I became a senior in high school. College was better, but not by much."

Samantha handed her a big, pottery bowl of salad to put on the table with matching place settings. Laryn gingerly carried it in her left arm. Her mother went all out for Italian dinners. Colorful salad bowls were by each plate. The homemade dressing made of oil and vinegar reeked of garlic. Laryn's mouth drooled.

When Samantha decided the dinner was ready, she instructed Laryn to call the fellows.

She entered the living room and all eyes went to her. It was a heady feeling to have both Quinn and Billy looking at her as if she was dessert. She announced, "Dinner is ready."

All eyes went to the door to the dining room. They arose as a unit and headed to the door. Boy did that blow her idea that they were looking at her.

She had to get out of the way or be run over by the mob. Quinn did kiss her cheek as he went by. Billy patted her on the head as he was taller than her. Dayne and her dad didn't even look at her as they passed.

Jordan indicated a place for Bill, as he preferred to be called. He motioned that Laryn should sit next to him. That left Dayne and Quinn on the other side of the table. Quinn looked surprised at the seating arrangements. On other Sunday dinners Laryn had always sat next to him.

He gave the other man a steely look that went right over Bill's head. Laryn watched the byplay and wondered if Quinn was getting interested in her. A few kisses did not make a relationship in her estimation.

Samantha brought in a tray with two casseroles of lasagna. One chicken and one vegetarian and both would be delicious thought Laryn. The dinner went well, but it did seem as if Billy had come to dinner to see Dayne and catch up on the good-old-days in high school.

They had their usual game of one-on-one basketball out in the driveway, which Laryn watched and used the excuse that she'd have to change clothes. To be truthful, she hurt too much from the near-miss bullet to even try.

When Billy left, Laryn accompanied him out the door.

Quinn kept looking towards the door after an extended time had elapsed. What she saw in that over-muscled oaf he couldn't imagine. When Laryn came back in, Quinn commented. "Hey pretty lady, come sit down and tell me how your week went. I haven't seen you lately at the gym."

Laryn went and sat down by Quinn on the couch. He put his arm around the back to make more room and grabbed her left hand putting it on his leg beside her. His muscles rippled as he squirreled around some in the process. Laryn's mood improved. She felt like leaning into him, but this was her parent's house and a general conversation was in progress.

It was fun learning what had happened since the last Sunday dinner when they were all together. It was more than fun having her hand on that thigh in the Chino-slick pants. Periodically, Quinn would whisper something in her ear that pertained to the conversation that would make her smile and her dangly earrings quiver from the sensation. Life could be good.

Eventually Quinn had to leave. He had things that needed doing on his days off that couldn't be put off forever. He kissed Laryn on the cheek as he arose to go.

"I hope to see you around this week, lovely lady."

Laryn grinned at him. "I'll try my best, kind sir."

Laryn joined her mother in the kitchen getting another round of coffee and putting a few chocolate chip cookies on a tray.

Samantha asked, "Well, how did it go with Bill Butler after dinner?"

Laryn looked dejected. "I really think he came to see Dayne and talk sports with the men. He didn't even notice me or compliment me on how I look these days. He didn't ask me for a phone number or a date."

Samantha put her arm around her daughter. "That's all right, sweetie. Quinn looked like he was jealous. Is anything going on there?"

She looked at her mother with sad eyes. "I'm not sure. I like Quinn a lot. He's so focused on his career I'm not sure that I'm anything but a patron to him. We did watch a movie together at my apartment and he kissed me on the cheek just now." Laryn's eyes brightened. "That's the first sign I've had that he might be more interested in me than just a patron of his gym."

Samantha grimaced, "Oh, honey, I'm sorry. I like Quinn a lot, too. He fits right in with this family. From what I can deduce, he doesn't know much about family life and is trying to come to terms with how things work, both smoothly and the yelling part."

Her Mother laughed a girlish laugh which belied her age. Being a writer made her more astute about life than she looked. She hated her blonde, tiny bimbo look. Most people didn't take her seriously. She reflected that as she gently patted her daughter on the back.

"I love you, Mom. You can make me come out of my *feel-sorry-for-myself* mood quicker than anyone I know. Is it because you're my mom, or is it because you're a writer, or is it because you're a pip-squeak and have had to put up with a lot of issues during your long, old life?"

"Watch that *'old'* part, dear, or I'll be forced to call your dad in to take you out to the woodshed and deliver the old what-for to your behind."

Laryn reached down and hugged her mother. "It's time for me to leave and get something done down at my place. I probably need to change the water in my fish bowl and water the ivy plant."

"Good excuse since I know all about your fake fish, but I love you anyway." She kissed Laryn on the cheek and swatted her bottom as she left the kitchen.

Quinn reflected on his visit to the Scott residence as he loaded towels into the industrial washing machine. This was the second time Laryn had brought a fellow home for the Sunday dinner ritual. Was this a custom at their house, or was Laryn trying to make him jealous? Was he getting a big head for even thinking she was interested in him? He was just her trainer at the physical fitness center.

He leaned against the washer as he started the cycle. If felt warm to his suddenly cool body. His thoughts continued. Yeah, they had had a pizza and a movie and he had kissed her mouth by accidental design as he had left her apartment. He was starting to get annoyed when she brought someone new to the dinner table. Did that mean he wanted more from her?

He hadn't had a girlfriend in so long he wasn't sure that was the right word even. After his military tour was over, he had hit the '*Muscleman*' contest circuit. Women and girls did hang on you then, but that was just groupie adoration. Having no family to model his ideas of family life after, he hadn't thought in terms of getting serious about anyone.

Now, the thought of Laryn getting involved with another man felt like a betrayal. It wasn't of course, because she didn't even know he was interested in her. He was sure she thought of him only as her exercise guy, or even his place as a quiet place to go to blow-off steam from her hectic job.

The machine started to bump and swirl the towels around. He walked away from it and surveyed the exercise room. Everything was under control. Tim, an older guy, who took over when he needed a day off, was talking and laughing at a group of oldie-but-goodie fellows that were kind of like groupies to him. Quinn, himself, didn't see these fellows much. They were Tim's friends.

He walked back to his office. He'd put the towels in the dryer after awhile. Now, he needed a plan to get Laryn to like him more than all those yahoos she was bringing home to the Sunday dinners.

Next time he saw her, he'd ask her what things she'd like to do and when was her next day off. He'd start getting into her head. He knew she was a junk-food addict, but made good choices when she could. She loved old movies and hated the over-sexed ones. He didn't know her taste in music or what she thought were fun things to do.

God, he hoped she didn't love ballet or the opera. He could take some of the opera music, but to have to watch either one didn't seem very manly to him. Although he wasn't interested in art, he could go to an art museum and enjoy it. You could see weird things in some pictures he was sure the artist hadn't painted there, like a dinosaur in the shadows on a sidewalk or a pirate's face in a mountain range. It was a perverse view of art, but imaginative, he preened to himself.

Quinn realized he was lacking in refinement. A good walk or run on a beach was more his style, but if he had to, he could learn other things. Maybe to start with he would take her to a local tavern with good music to listen to and even dance. He could dance and gyrate and if he had to, take off he clothes. Musclemen weren't dummies when it came to earning money or fascinating the ladies with their talents. He laughed an evil laugh and twirled a non-existent mustache as he left to put the towels in the dryer.

ON AND OFF THE BEAT #20

Laryn was sitting at her desk when a call came in through Harve at the front desk.

"Hello. This is Officer Scott. How may I help you?"

"This is Mrs. Anderson. My husband was the one you found in the barn in eastern Washington."

"Sure, I remember. Again, what can I do for you?"

"Well, I just wanted to report to you the findings they did on the investigation into his death. Evidently, he was going to throw hay down to the animals when he may have encountered the cougar. The blood on the pitchfork was blood from the cat species. They presume he forked the cat as it charged and the impact may have off-balanced him and he fell grabbing the hoist rope, which tangled around his neck breaking it. He died instantly."

Laryn responded, "I'm so sorry for your loss, Mrs. Anderson."

"Thank you, Officer Scott. It was a comfort having you there when we found him. I just wanted you to know what had happened. I'm glad he didn't choke to death. It was quick for him."

Laryn admired the lady for her strength in losing her husband. "Will you be all right? It must be hard to be alone and raise your young daughter by yourself."

"Denny left me an insurance policy. He was on the road so much and worried something would happen to him. It was strange the accident happened at home and not on the road. That's why they did an investigation on his death. They wanted to make sure it was an accident for the insurance company."

"Well, I'm glad thing have worked out for you and your daughter, Mrs. Anderson."

"Thank you again for all your help, Officer Scott. I just wanted you to know. Good bye for now."

Laryn leaned back in her chair. What a strange call. No one ever thanked a police office for their help. Usually, you were yelled at, spit at or they vowed to sue you, the department and the whole state.

It felt good to be acknowledged. She went back to work. Reports! Reports! Reports!

Quinn Madden wasn't off duty yet but he knew Laryn was, so he called her.

"Laryn, my lovely lady, is there any chance I could come over after work tonight? You realize it couldn't be until after nine-thirty tonight, which I know is late."

"Sure, Quinn. I don't go to bed until after the news. Come on over."

"You don't even want to know why I want to come? You're a trusting soul aren't you?"

"I'm a police officer. Try something funny and you'll end up looking at my carpet, fellow."

He chuckled. He didn't doubt it in the least that she would take an invader down. She'd already threatened him when he brought pizza the last time. "Could I bring something to eat while you watch your favorite program, like decadent ice cream?"

"Oooooh," she cooed over the phone. *"Double fudge ripple would hit the spot and a bloody movie on TV,"*

Quinn rolled his eyes. He'd asked for that kind of retaliation. "How about twice whipped double fudge ripple? It has less calories in it."

"I can hardly wait, big guy."

"See ya soon, girl."

He wanted to hurry and close the club down, but that was not how the work went around here. You did your job or lose clients. It was just that he had a plan to woo Laryn and wanted to implement it before he chickened out. He went about his job helping people with bottled water, how to work on a problem area for their body, but his mind was on Laryn and her double fudge ripple ice cream and sensuously licking the spoon after each bite

Quinn knocked on Laryn's door. She opened it immediately and dragged him into the room. Seeing the package she grabbed it from him and laid a big smacking kiss on his cheek.

"You lovely man, you."

Quinn stood with his mouth literally hanging open. "Are you glad to see me or is it the ice cream?"

Giving him a flirty grin, she answered, "Both, silly man. At this moment, I love you both about the same; one for the richness and you for your thoughtfulness."

She talked as she dished them both up a bowl. Handing him his dish, she took hers over and sat down on the couch. "Have a seat. I'm watching that new Hannibal series. You have the feeling at any moment he's going to eat someone even behind bars."

"My Lord, woman, you are a blood thirsty type and while you're eating ice cream, too."

Laryn looked at him. She grinned, "It's only fiction, Quinn. Just fiction! Real life would bring me to attention and maybe even have my gun drawn for instant action."

He gave her a quizzical glance. "All right then," and he sat down beside her. Very close beside her. Rubbing shoulders close to her. She glanced at him, but went back to spooning ice cream slowly into her mouth, then, slowly turning the spoon over, licking the bowl of it each time just as he imagined she would do.

He was glad he had his pleated Docker pants on as it had room to expand his body's private parts. He turned to the program on TV. It was not as bad a show as Laryn had predicted. He'd wait for the commercials to talk to her about her likes and dislikes. He would get to know her better besides Laryn's working side and her time at his gym. At her parents' Sunday dinners, he only got the familie's view of Laryn.

Finally a commercial.

"Laryn, what do you like to do on your days off besides go to Sunday dinner at your folks?"

She quit sucking on her spoon and looked at him. "I hardly do anything. I've lost track of most of my girl friends, I don't mix with my cohorts at work. I don't go to the movies because they will eventually come on TV. I wash clothes, clean the apartment, water my ivy and change water in my fish bowl." She stuck up her finger. "Oh! I read a book sometimes." She grinned again. "A gory murder mystery!"

He laughed. "Of course it would be gory. How about the next time you have a day off, you let me know so I can get the time off and we'll go to a bar with music and we'll dance a little or karaoke a bit?"

Having taken another bite, she slowly took the spoon off her tongue and moving just her wrist as she pointed it at him. "You mean you and me?" The spoon swiveled first towards him and then her.

He nodded his head. ""Yeah, you and me."

She took another bite of ice cream, swiveling the spoon as she licked it like she'd been doing, his pants jerked to attention again, then she turned and looked at him once more.

"Okay."

Quinn grinned, "That's all you've got to say is 'okay'"

He threw his head back and closed his eyes for a second and thought; *Thank God, saved from the ballet date.*

Smiling wide, she cocked her head at him. "I'd love to go out with you any time and anywhere, Quinn. Is that all right with you?"

He leaned over and kissed her ice cream tasting lips and replied, "Great!" then turned back to watch the program she had on her TV.

Laryn had just gotten off work and was fixing her supper of grilled cheese sandwich and tomato bisque soup when her cell phone rang. Removing her food from the stove, she answered on the third ring.

"This is Maria Hernandez's mother."

"Oh, how nice to hear from you, how was Maria's trip?"

"Well, that's why I'm calling. Have you heard from her? We've had no word since she got to Disneyland. She was very excited and had even been to the beach down there."

Laryn was concerned. "No, I've not heard from her. Now, I'm worried, too. Was she still with *Anywhere Trucking*?"

"Yes. She said Bubba was being really good to her and she was having a good time. She did say they were taking a load of something to Mexico and was glad she had taken her passport."

Laryn thought a moment. "So you think they might have gone into Mexico?"

'It sounds reasonable to me, but she should have contacted me by now and that's why I called you to see if you had heard from her."

Still playing the part of Maria's friend, Laryn said, "Darn it! No I haven't and I so wanted to hear about her trip. Maybe her cell phone doesn't work in Mexico. What are you going to do since she hasn't called in?"

Maria's mother sounded worried. *"You could be right about her phone. I think I'll wait a few more days and then I'm reporting her missing. I don't know how to get in touch with the California missing persons or anyone in Mexico. I just don't know what to do."*

Laryn could hear the trembling in her voice. She was probably crying. Laryn was more frightened for Maria than wanting to cry, but she had to keep her cool.

"Mrs. Hernandez, I think you would be wise to call the police and let them worry about how to contact California and Mexico. They would know the number of the Mexican Consulate, too"

Maria's mother seemed to brace herself up. *"That's a good idea. Thank you for the advice. You're a good friend to worry about my Maria. Please call me if you hear anything from her."*

"I will, Mrs. Hernandez. Bye for now."

Layrn felt guilty for her deception, but she had the information she needed to go forword on the investigation into the disappearance of Latina girls. Still, why Latina girls only?"

Her supper was cold. She re-warmed her soup and just made some toast to go with it. The smell was tangy and made her mouth water. With the trauma of what she'd just heard, it went down smoothly and was what she needed right now.

Sitting at her retro table and glancing out at the deceptively slow moving Skagit River, she contemplated all that she had learned. Two missing girls were two too many. It was time to get the detectives involved further.

She might be raked over the coals for her part in the investigation, but that wasn't important in the scheme of things when someone's life might be in danger or even lost.

ON AND OFF THE BEAT #21

The next day at work, Laryn called Detectives Fenton and Smith. Luckily, Smith answered. Even thought Smith wasn't happy with her, she'd rather talk to a woman at this point, than a man.

"Detective Smith, this is Officer Scott. I think you need to come over to my office. I have more information on Maya Toreno and maybe another missing Latina girl."

Detective Smith sounded in rare, meaning bloody, form again. *And why do you think another Latina girl is missing? Why are you picking on only Latina girls?*

Laryn wanted to shudder at the caustic voice on the line, but she was a police officer and had just as much right to do investigating in her jurisdiction as the detectives.

"I'm not picking on Latina girls and I'm just as interested in knowing why these girls are missing and not other nationalities. Maya is my friend and the other girl was questioned on a routine truck stop our department did a while back. If you will come over to my office I'll bring you up-to-date on what I know and see if you think it's important or not to this case." Laryn hoped she had appeased Detective Smith on asking for her advice.

It worked.

"Okay, we'll be there in about fifteen minutes. Will that fit into your schedule?"

"Sure. I'll have all my information laid out for you." Whew, thought Laryn, wiping her forehead. The first part was over, now if she could just keep her cool while she explained her part in the investigation.

Within the requisite fifteen minutes, an unmarked car screeched to halt out in the parking lot. In walked the two detectives and asked Harve where Officer Scott was. Even though, Harve knew that Laryn was expecting them, he still stalled and buzzed her office area. He felt they were being a little uppity in their manner. It wouldn't hurt them to learn a little humility in dealing with people that were only trying to help other people in this line of work.

"She's in," he told them and went over to the half-door and let them in and motioned towards the back region of the building. They had been there before, so had no problem finding Laryn.

Her office was just a cubicle, but she treasured it. Her family's picture was in a corner slot. There was a Valentine heart on a bulletin board left over from an office party and post-its notes galore.

She indicated seats for the two detectives. They each took one and looked at her waiting for the show to begin. Laryn had her papers all ready for her presentation. So she began at the beginning, again to set any record straight that the two detectives might have misconstrued.

"I got the call this strange call on my telephone at home that someone was about to be murdered. As you know, that started my curiosity and investigation. It ended up the only friend that was missing was Maya Toreno. I checked the truck stop where the truckers eat and Maya worked. A fellow named Bubba seemed to be the one she went with.

"Mr. Toreno didn't know any of this information, so I did some surveillance on my own and came up with a trucker named Bubba with a trucking line called *Anywhere Trucking Company.*

"Our department needed to do a yearly check on compliance, so we did a routine truck stop checking them off on our compliance sheet. While Officer Renaldo questioned a driver named Earl Bubdecker, nicknamed Bubba, with *Anywhere Trucking,* I talked with the Latina girl he had with him. Her name is Maria Hernandez from Ferndale. Bubba was taking her to Disneyland in California. This was the same story Maya told her co-workers. It turned out both girls had their passports with them. Do you have any questions so far?"

Detective Fenton nodded his head. "Yeah, what does this have to do with our dead girl out at the Toreno house?"

Laryn shook her head. "I don't know, but I think something is going on with Bubba taking Latina girls to California and maybe on to Mexico. Could be the unidentified girl was from Mexico and that is why no one had come forward to claim the body."

With a smile on her face, Detective Smith commented, "We didn't think of that. We presumed the parents might not have wanted to be deported. They still may come forward eventually. We're doing a sketch of what she may have looked like and will post her picture and further details now that we don't think Mr. Toreno had anything to do with her death. It seemed like natural causes from her diabetes."

Laryn was elated to hear that news. Mr. Toreno was off the hook but his Maya was still missing and no one seemed to care, but her and she needed help, too.

In his gruff voice, Detective Fenton asked, "Could we have the information you have collected?" He looked at his partner, "We'll add it to ours and see what we can come up with. I think you're right to be concerned. It could be a sex-trafficking trade we know nothing about and the girls will have been conned into going with the fellow with his bait of a promise of a Disneyland adventure."

Laryn nodded, "You could be right. The Hernandezes from Ferndale are about to contact the police within days because they are worried, too. I'm to call them if I hear from Maria."

"Okay, you call us if you hear from her, too. We'll keep you informed of our investigation." Fenton gathered up the papers Laryn had copied for him and stuck them back in the file folder she had handed him.

Laryn thankfully had help now. They could get out into the outer world when her hands were tied to the city of Mount Vernon.

Detective Fenton and Smith entered their vehicle. Fenton drove while they both contemplated the information that was given to them.

Fenton spoke first. "When we get back to our office, we'll evaluate what we've been give by Officer Scott."

"Sure, Jasper, I agree. Laryn did give us a lot of clues."

"Laryn?"

"Yeah, that's Officer Scott's name." She smirked, "Like mines' Trudie and yours is Jasper."

Fenton looked quickly at her with his dead-panned face. "Ha! Ha! I don't think that's funny. We're talking investigation here."

"I know, but in talking among ourselves, Officer Scott is a longer word than Laryn."

"That was two words."

Trudie shook her head. "You are so anal, Jasper. You're the one who got us off on another subject. Laryn did give us a lot of information. Get over it."

Jasper snorted. "Do you think it's enough for an A.P.B.?"

Trudie glanced at him. "I don't know. An all points bulletin and a warrant go hand-in-hand. We'll need to get all the facts together before we can approach a judge for a warrant. I do think it will come to that." She paused, "Let's hope no more girls go missing while we contemplate the matter."

"You are so right. Damn, it takes so long to check out each point needed to slam-dunk a jackass."

They continued on to their office.

Laryn was at home just finishing doing her supper dishes when the phone rang. It was from her police station and urgent. A span of the bridge, that crossed the mighty Skagit River, had collapsed, throwing a car and a truck with a camper into the water. There even may be more cars in the water, but not visible like those two were. All hands on deck were the orders. Use alternate routes to get to the police station. Traffic had been diverted to Old 99 which went through downtown old Mount Vernon.

Laryn grabbed clean clothes and in her car headed to the nearest stop light that would get her across Old 99 and up towards east Mount Vernon and then north to the police station. Crossing at the light, she could see huge trucks making their way through the congested two way street.

At the station, chaos rained. Natalie, who took Harve's place after his shift, was inundated with calls from worried people about their loved ones who should have been home by now, and were they in the river?

Natalie handed her a paper while she answered questions on the phone. The orders were for Laryn to help with crowd control on the south side of the bridge. On-lookers were out in force and in danger of crowding each other into the river, adding to more rescues. She hurriedly changed into her uniform and grabbed a camera. With no police cars available to use, she took off running to find a shortcut to the dikes along the river. The railroad tracks were her best bet.

She didn't get a view of the broken bridge on I-5 until she crossed under the new Old 99 Bridge. The sight was awe inspiring. She could see a car in the water from where she stood and a guy was on the roof of his vehicle. The span had crumpled close to the north end and had plunged into the river. Only the upper broken trusses were showing above the water, too high up for anyone to climb as a form of escape.

The gravel sides of the dikes were steep, but people were standing and sitting on them with many more standing on the wide area at the top. Cameras were out and in the waning light, capturing the historic event before their eyes.

The river's look was deceiving as it was calm and peaceful above the surface, but was known to have a strong current beneath. It looked like a bed of silver in the twilight of the evening; beautiful, chaotic and dangerous.

Since she hadn't gotten her orders yet, she could only ask people to keep back from the river. She worked her way over to another officer and asked him what their orders were.

Officer Burke answered, "I didn't get direct orders either. Everyone is too busy. My advice is to just walk along the bank here and be alert to anyone flirting with danger and react accordingly."

Laryn nodded and turned back the way she had come. Just her presence might help control a problem. Pushing and shoving was dangerous, as there were small children on the steep side of the dike, yelling observations was, natural but arguing loudly was a sign of trouble.

Across on the other side of the river the town of Burlington butted up against it. The Burlington Police Department was doing their duty just as she was. Also, the state patrol and the county sheriff's department all had jobs. A quick thought for Laryn, was the rest of the county too busy watching the action to burglarize or have car accidents?

Laryn did her duty until well into the night as rescue squads got the survivors off of the top of the car. Seemingly, they had somehow gotten on top of one car. Divers were scanning underwater near the bridge in case there were more cars in the water. Heavy duty lights had been brought in for all this after dark activity. Workers created long shadows as they did their jobs. The scene now resembled ghosts as they entered and receded from the lights.

Sometimes, Laryn just gawked like the rest of the crowd. She snapped pictures accordingly. It wasn't every day you got to witness first hand all these different groups in action; rescue boasts, divers, ambulances on stand-by, police on both sides of the river and huge trucks with cranes to help with the salvage. It was both awe inspiring and frightening at the same time.

Such a miracle that no one was killed and only two vehicles went into the water. Seven o'clock at night was usually a busy time on this interstate highway. God must have been riding with the many commuters in His care.

Laryn left her duty station without orders when most of the audience had gone and anyone left was up on the road of the dike. She walked back to the Mount Vernon station the way she had come.

She hated to think what the officers that had been on traffic duty had had to contend with. Intersections were a problem by being blocked between light changes from the cars and trucks. She knew that some lights were only a long truck apart and naturally the cars' drivers were in a hurry to get to wherever they were going. Until the bridge was fixed it would be a long day for all the officers directing traffic.

At the station, she found out the truck that supposedly did the damage had stopped right away and had been as horrified as the rest of the people at what had happened. He didn't think it was his fault a nudge of this trailer had done all that damage, but of course there would be an investigation into the accident.

Harve was back on the desk and taking turns with Natalie to field telephone calls. Here it was still pretty hectic. Officers coming off duty were explaining their experiences of the evening. Laryn joined in as some hadn't even seen the bridge mess. She hadn't been involved with the traffic and Harve, on the desk, had listened to many interesting calls, with some off the wall, complaining that their dog wouldn't stop howling, so there must be someone dead in the river. A call-back was a women saying her drunken husband was home and hadn't gone in the river, but now she wished he had, the no-good-son-of-a-bitch.

Laryn was home now and so tired she was sure to sleep tonight. She'd better as they were all promised overtime and nose to the grindstone until the bridge was temporarily fixed as promised by the governor of the state of Washington.

Wow! The governor had been somewhere on the bridge overlooking the damage. Laryn retired to her bedroom for what was left of the night.

ON AND OFF THE BEAT #22

Laryn had endured a tense two weeks. She was exhausted, as were most of the employees of the county. Laryn had worked different shifts to spell officers assigned to traffic duty. She was home and too tired to eat, or even sleep.

There was a knock on her door. Damn, she'd have to get up to answer it. She looked out the peep-hole in the door. All she saw was a pot with a lid on it. She opened the door wide as Quinn came in bearing a pot of something that smelled good.

As he passed, he leaned in and kissed her cheek. "Hi, pretty lady, long time no see."

He pressed on to her stove, turned on the burner to low and came back to the room to observe her. She still held the door open. "You can close the door now," he grinned at her.

Laryn closed the door. She was glad to see him, but so tired she could hardly speak. "What are you doing here at this ungodly hour?"

"Hey, it's only eleven o'clock on a Sunday evening. Your folks had me over for dinner and I was instructed to bring this pot of stew to you along with homemade bread to dip into it. In fact, since that was this afternoon, I'm kind of hungry, too."

Laryn plopped down on her couch. "I'm too tired to eat."

Quinn came over and sat down beside her. Grabbing up the remote control for the TV, he turned it on. "You can watch the news while I get everything ready. I'll even spoon it into your mouth if necessary."

The usual news about the Skagit Bridge was reiterated by the Seattle newscasters. If it wasn't for the news, she might not know what was going on. Nose to the grindstone was about it.

"You might have to. If I can't lift my arms to my mouth, I might have to pig-eat-it and if I do that I might fall asleep and fall face first into it and drown. It's too dangerous for me to eat."

Chuckling, Quinn patted her on the head. Her hair felt like straw from sweating under her cap. "You poor thing. I'll take care of you. Now don't fall asleep while I cut the bread and get the bowls out."

The TV went on about a murder case on trial in Florida. She glanced over at Quinn. He looked so good to her tired eyes and when he sat beside her, he smelled fresh and clean. She smelled like sweat and exhaust fumes. Her feet hurt and her eyes burned.

The TV continued to blare. A child fell out of an open window in a third floor apartment. That perked her ears up for a second. The child was taken to a hospital, but its injuries were considered non-life threatening.

Quinn came over to her. "Can you come to the table or do you want to eat right here?" He motioned to the coffee table in front of the couch.

"I'll come to the table. Getting up is halfway to taking a shower to go to bed."

Quinn took her hand and pulled, helping her to her feet. If she hadn't been so tired he might have pulled her into his arms and kissed her a good warm-blooded kiss. As it was, he was here to help keep her alive, as her mother had instructed.

He pushed her chair in for her and put a paper napkin on her lap. He ladled up a bowl of the Mexican meatball soup, full of vegetables and healthful juices. He crushed a few corn chips into it and handed her a spoon.

"Eat!" he ordered.

After the first bite had hit her mouth and the slightly spicy juices invaded it, she perked up.

"Ohhhh, this is so good." She closed her eyes in appreciation.

Quinn noticed and in alarm, said, "Now don't go to sleep on me. You have to change your clothes and maybe even bathe before you go to sleep. I don't know your ritual, but I'm willing to learn." He grinned at his private thoughts about her rituals and how he might fit in.

Laryn dipped her bread in the juices and bit it off. "I'm starting to wake up. I guess I really needed this and the attention of a handsome man helps a lot, too." She smiled at him, the first sign of life she had given him since he came in bearing gifts.

Enthusiastically, he raised his arms, "Thank God, she lives." His theatrical antics made her laugh out loud. "That's my girl. You'll live to fight another day directing traffic." He ended this sentence drolly.

He had just taken a few bites of his soup when he jumped up again. "I'm going to run you a bath while you finish eating."

"I don't want to bathe, I want to shower."

"You need to soak your muscles first then you can shower."

She cocked her head at him, "Awwww, my own personal trainer. How did I get so luck as to get a handsome fellow like you instead of that old guy at your gym?"

"When I can sit on your back and rub lavender oil into your shoulders and muscles, you'll know why I'm your personal trainer." Quinn quickly left to go fill her tub.

Laryn's eyes opened wide. "Wow!" was the most she could come up with and bent her head to continue eating, a thoughtful look on her face.

When she had finished eating, she went to her bedroom to get her shorts and a tank top to sleep in and a housecoat. She didn't know if Quinn would be here when she finished getting ready for bed or not, but she sure wouldn't run around in her pajamas. After Quinn's announcement of wanting to give her a back rub, her sleep-wear was too suggestive to be seen in. Later she could analyze his remark when she wasn't so tired.

Quinn left her to her bath and shower. He told her he would clean up the kitchen and wait until she came back out before going home. He put the rest of the cooled soup into individual containers he found in her cabinets with enough for one meal each. The bread went into a baggy.

Still having time on his hands, he changed the water in her fish bowl, washing it out first as it had started to get green algae. He added water to her live ivy plant. He wasn't such a neat-freak to dust or vacuum her place. As long as you didn't run your finger over a shelf, they didn't look dusty. He knew this from his own nearly bare apartment.

She came out of the bathroom with the scent of roses following her. She looked tousled and sleepy. He ambled over to her and took her in his arms and kissed her soundly. Now she looked soundly kissed, tousled and sleepy, just the way he would like to remember her as he left to go home.

"See you soon, lovely lady." He shut the door behind him.

A month of hard work and overtime was behind her. The temporary bridge span was in place and except for oversized trucks, everything was back to normal. The businesses had taken quite a hit because the locals had kept away from Mount Vernon and Burlington with all the traffic problems.

Laryn had two days off and visited her family first. As soon as Quinn heard she was free, he called her at her apartment.

"I hear you have two days off."

So glad to hear from him, Laryn quipped, "Who told you that?"

Quinn could almost hear her smile. *"I'd say a little bird, but he's big enough to be a condor. An eagle is too stately."*

Laryn did laugh then. With her cell phone to her ear, she went over to her table to sit down while she talked. The view through the window showed the Skagit River flowing soothingly by. "I might have known my loud-mouth brother is a gossip. But I love him just the same. I'm almost giddy with the freedom of a few days off."

Quinn would have liked to continue talking with her, but he was on duty and he needed to make arrangements for a date if she was willing. *"How would you like to go out tomorrow night? I'll get off early and we can go to my favorite tavern and listen to a great band and dance a few numbers. They even have good food. We could leave early enough to eat before the band starts to play. I don't drink, so you don't have to worry about me driving home."*

Laryn was thoughtful. Quinn was trying too hard to get her to go on a date with him. What was his problem? "I'd love to go out with you, Quinn, but why are you trying so hard to convince me to go out with you? I've never seen you do anything to make me refuse to be seen with a handsome hunk."

Quinn wiped his hand over his face. *"It's a carry-over from the circuit days. Groupies followed us everywhere. If you didn't have an entourage of at least two on your arm, you were considered second place. The competition was great but I hated being seen as a player. It made me hide in my room and not come out until the next trial. Of course then you were considered gay and I didn't like that either since I wasn't."*

Laryn giggled, "Well, Quinn, if you promise to keep your clothes on I'd love to go out with you and if they think I'm a groupie and you're a player we'll just prove them right. I'll hang onto you the next time we go out."

"Awwww, there will be a next time! That's so sweet of you."

"Quinn, I've never been called sweet in my life. Why do you think I'm considered to be a good cop? I take no nonsense from anyone."

Quinn barked a laugh. *"That includes me, too. I have to go. We'll try for seven. Dress for a tavern."* He hung up.

The next day Laryn cleaned her place and washed underclothes and pajamas. That was all that was dirty from her month on overtime. Who had time to do anything but go to bed? Her uniforms she had cleaned and shirts were done by a laundry where sharp creases were put in them. They would need to be picked up this next week.

She'd even lost some weight, but wasn't going to tell her mother that. Quinn probably wouldn't approve either. It was one thing to diet, but another to lose weight because you were too tired to eat. It showed you can stay alive by drinking lots of water.

She showered and curled her front bangs. She needed a haircut, but for a woman, she was still in style with hair reaching her shoulders. Her blue jeans were a little loose, but her rhinestones T-shirt didn't look too bad. In sea blue color and '*BAD TO* THE *BONE*' in script lettering emblazed across the front, it looked both attractive and was a good color for her blonde Nordic self. But she groaned looking at her feet as her toenails needed to be painted. No sandals for her. Her ballerinas would work. They felt so comfortable she moaned with delight when she put them on. Her feet had been in boots for so long she felt like she could do a pirouette in her ballerinas and look graceful.

If Quinn didn't cringe when he saw her, she would go out with her feelings high and her ego tripping over itself hanging on handsome Quinn's arm.

Quinn picked her up right on time. He took one look at her and certainly didn't cringe.

"My God woman, you are so beautiful I'll have to fight off all the men in the joint to just dance with you a few times." Then he kissed her soundly.

Laryn sighed. "You don't have to worry. I'll just decline any overtures and hang on you like the groupies would like to do. Besides, I've never had to beat off men in my whole life."

Quinn cocked his head. "Well, there is a first time for everything, but I hope this isn't it. I want your undivided attention and get to know you outside the gym and your family." He grabbed her coat from the back of the couch. "Let's go."

Laryn slung her tiny hanging chain purse over her shoulders and off they went.

The pub was cute and the music loud and western. They ordered iced tea in mugs with a twist of lemon. Neither had a straw to drink with. It looked like they had beer, but didn't have to worry about it going stale while they danced. Due to the loud music, they didn't talk too much.

Quinn held her hand on the table and pulled her close to say something. They ate delicious hamburgers, with a green salad for their health. Okay, so Quinn didn't complain about the hamburgers, he was just glad she was eating with gusto.

Again, he was surprised. She was a great dancer. She almost read his mind. When he'd gyro, she did, too. She could spin on a dime. If he took a long step, she didn't even stumble. But the slow dancing, that he'd never enjoyed before, became his favorite. Hugging her close, body to body and moving her legs with his, was so erotic he felt like losing it a few time and heading for his blazer and the path for home. There was no danger of her becoming his groupie, he was becoming her groupie.

They headed home before the band quit for the night. Laryn had to work the next day and far be it from him to keep her from the needed sleep.

Laryn turned in the comfortable seat of the blazer. "I enjoyed this evening so much. Thank you, Quinn, for taking me dancing. I think the last time I danced was with my girl friends at an all-night party in college. We didn't drink tea then and I remember having a terrible headache the next day." She smiled remembering that night. "Goes to show, you don't have to drink or use drugs to have a good time." She again turned to him. "You just have to have a good partner."

Quinn glanced back at her. "And I'm the one who had the best partner and I didn't have to take my clothes off either."

Laryn laughed a tinkling sound, most unlike her. "I could arrange to have you take your clothes off yet. The evening isn't over."

Quinn pretended outrage. "Laryn Scott, what would your mother think if I took my clothes off on our first date?"

Laryn pretended to give it some thought, her finger creating a dimple in her cheek. "You're right. She would be spouting the *Birds-and-Bees* talk again." She grinned at him. "Maybe next time I'll get your clothes off you."

They arrived at her place. He leaned over and kissed her. "I won't come up. It's too tempting and maybe next time I will let you take off my clothes."

Laryn opened the door and climbed out. Her come-hither, parting shot was, "We'll see."

ON AND OFF THE BEAT #23

Laryn was again sitting at her desk. Her butt hadn't been there since the Skagit Bridge collapsed. Since she hadn't written anyone up for an infraction, she didn't have a lot of catching up to do. Her desk chair felt good as she squirreled around in it. She'd never noticed that before. The cubical even felt like home. Nothing like a month off your regular schedule to make you appreciate the normal one again. Later she would do her rounds of all the schools to see if any drug trafficking was going on. Both college and high school had a knack for trafficking when the police officers were busy elsewhere.

Her phone rang. "Officer Scott speaking. How may I help you?"

"This is Detective Smith." A pleasant feminine voice said. *"I've got some news for you. Detective Fenton didn't think we needed to let you know what had happened in the Toreno case, but I know Maya was a friend of yours, so I felt you deserved an update."*

Laryn's heart began to beat frantically. 'You've learned something new about the case?"

Smith laughed. *"Well nothing really new, but we've got Bubba in custody and he's blathering like a prisoner held with a cattle prod, although you realize we never use cattle prods, but I watch a lot of police shows and the bad guys use them to get information."* Again a laugh, *"Now I'm blathering."*

Laryn laughed, too, from excitement. "That's okay, just tell me what's going on and if it's good news I can tell Mr. Toreno."

"Well, Bubba was picked up with another Latina girl and he told us he has been taking Latina girls to Mexico, but they are all over twenty-one and it was their idea. He claims he told them where to meet him if they wanted a ride back and none of them did, so he got another load of stuff to bring back to the states and home he went."

"Why that dirty so-and-so. Maya would never leave her father up here alone and the Hernandezes from Ferndale have been expecting a call from their daughter and it hasn't happened. There's more to the story than that, don't you think?"

"Yes, I think there is and we are waiting for a search order for his truck. There's been a lot of girls in that truck. Bubba doesn't know what we know, so is spilling a lot more information than we have knowledge of. He insists that he's never taken advantage of them. He enjoys the company on a long lonely haul and a promise of Disneyland gets them every time."

Laryn gulped. "He won't get off, will he?"

"We can hold him long enough to get that search warrant, but after that it's iffy."

"How about the dead girl out at the Toreno place? Does he know anything about that?" Laryn scratched her head in frustration. "Can I sit in on an interview with him?"

"I can ask and see what I can do. I've got to go now. Talk to you later."

Talk about excitement and frustration at the same time. Laryn felt she had it. She was torn between calling Mr. Toreno and waiting until she got an interview with Bubba. Bubba was doing more than just taking girls to Mexico out of the kindness of his heart. And the way he was talking to the detectives, he had taken more than the two she knew about.

The dead girl out at the Toreno place had died of a diabetic attack. She wasn't worried about her. It was too late for that, but it would be nice to at least inform her family of her death and the cause.

Bubba knew something and Laryn was determined to find out what that was. The nicest thing was that Maya and Maria might still be alive. They both spoke Spanish fluently and had job experience to get a job to tide them over. But, why hadn't they called home?

Laryn finished out her day with a patrol around the many schools with Farley Brunell. Nothing unusual happened so they went back to the station to go home for the night.

At home, Laryn made a BLT sandwich to go with her tomato soup. The bacon tasted so good, she felt she must have needed the salt. Getting salt for the hot weather was much better by eating bacon than taking a salt pill.

She'd just finished washing her few dishes when the phone rang.

"This is Trudie Smith again. We got the warrant and are working overtime to process the truck. We can only hold Bubba until ten o'clock tomorrow. If we don't have to turn him loose, you can come to the jail and listen to the continuing questioning."

Laryn was relieved. "I'll arrange to get the time off and I'll be there by nine o'clock. Maybe even an hour interview would help understand what might have happened?"

"See you tomorrow, then." Trudie Smith signed off.

Laryn was so excited that she had to tell someone. Usually that would be her Mother, but she hadn't told her family all about this case. Quinn was the one she wanted to talk to. He knew the most and even he didn't know much. It was after nine-thirty at night. He would be off duty at the Health Club.

She called him.

He answered.

"Quinn, I've got the best news on the Maya Toreno case. They have Bubba in custody until tomorrow at ten o'clock. I may get to talk to him."

She was so excited, he could hardly understand her.

"I take it you are excited about this information?" His deep chuckle calmed her down.

"Yes I am. It's the first time I haven't had to do the work on this case and they got information much faster than I was able to."

"Well, girl, you did most of the grunt work on the caset, so no wonder they got results so quickly."

She giggled, "Can I call you tomorrow? When I get excited, I don't know who to talk to, so I picked you. Mom would panic, Dad would give me unwanted advice and Dayne is just a jerky brother."

"Laryn, you may always call me anytime. It doesn't even have to be about your case, your jerky brother or your family."

"So I can just ruin your evening with talk?"

"You couldn't ruin my day no matter what. I enjoy talking to you. I prefer it face to face, but your voice is usually a pleasant break in my day. I say 'usually' because you are excited now and that gets me excited for you."

Laryn laid down on her couch, crossed her legs and settle in for a talk. "Okay, Quinn, I had a really good time on our date. You are a good dancer."

"Oh, I knew I could dance, but how do I kiss?"

"So, you are a fisherman, too."

He sounded confused, *"A fisherman?"*

Laryn laughed, "You're fishing for compliments. I think you are a wonderful kisser. I haven't had too much experience at kissing, but I'd rate you up there with the best if I was experienced."

"Well, I hope you don't go out there to get more experience just so you can rate me. I'd rather you just leave the kissing up to me and I'll even try to improve my technique."

"That sounds good. It means we will have to practice some more."

"It does. How about the next time you have a day off, you let me know ahead of time and I'll figure out some exciting thing to do and run it by you."

"Sounds good to me. I'll call you when I know more about the Toreno case or my day off. Good-bye for now." Laryn fanned her face. That was a heated conversation.

Quinn pumped his arm. He had a date with Laryn even if it was just a telephone call. He could hardly wait.

Laryn arrived at the jail about eight-thirty the next morning. She didn't want to miss whatever went down with Bubba. Even being a police officer, she had to go through the check point and prove she was what she said she was and her purpose for being there. She had nothing on her but her identification and her badge in her wallet.

She approved of the check point as there were so many kooks out there who could and would do anything to cause a problem. Laryn was met by both detectives.

Detective Fenton acknowledge her. "We're having Bubba brought into the interrogation room as we speak. This isn't an interrogation yet, but just a straight interview. If the truck provides any clues to what's going on so we can keep him longer, then we'll go into interrogation mode. Understand?"

Laryn nodded her head, afraid to speak in case she said the wrong thing and was kicked out. "I'm here to listen."

From their notepad, they reiterated what Bubba had told them yesterday after he and the girl had been picked up and his truck had been impounded.

They went into the interrogation room and reintroduced themselves to Bubba.

Detective Fenton started with, "Your name is Earl Bubdecker, also called Bubba, correct?"

Bubba nodded.

"You had a Latina girl with you when we did the traffic stop."

Bubba nodded.

"Could you speak the answers, so that they will be recorded?"

Again Bubba nodded then said, "Yes, and yes."

Detective Fenton carefully wrote the answer down next to the question. He would do this on each question presented to Bubba.

"And where were you taking her?"

"I told her I would take her to Disneyland if she would talk to me on the way to California. She said she would and she is over twenty one and I've never had sex with any of the girls I have taken to Disneyland. I have a wife in eastern Washington and would never step out on her." He snarled. "Anything else you want to know?"

Detective Fenton looked around his little group. "Do you know a Maya Toreno? Did you take her to California?"

Bubba nodded, "I think that was the name of a waitress at the truck stop and yes I took her to Disneyland and then she wanted to go on to Mexico with me. She didn't meet me back at the appointed time in Mexico and I have a timetable I need to stick to."

"So she was left in Mexico, but was healthy and alive the last time you saw her."

Bubba snorted, "Yes, she was alive and well and waved to me as she left to walk around."

"Was she going to visit relatives?"

"I have no idea. I had to get rid of my load that I took to Mexico and didn't walk around with her."

"Did she have her passport with her when you left her there on the street?"

Bubba looked around the room. If you watched his eyes, they looked shifty. He knew something and he wasn't going to tell them what it was. Both Laryn and Detective Smith noticed that and looked at each other and nodded.

Fenton noticed the two women nodded to each other. Something was wrong.

He had to get out of here to find out what the women knew or saw that he had missed. "Will you read over the questions and your answers and sign the paper if you have no objection to what we've asked you?"

Bubba was starting to squirm in his chair. "Sure, sure. I don't know what you guys are keeping me for. I have a load to pick up and need to be on my way."

He perused the paper Fenton had given him. The detective said, "If you'll just write, 'that is what I said' and sign your name, we'll get you out of here so you can collect your things and be on your way. This is in triplicate so I'll give you a copy of what we discussed."

Bubba signed the paper without comment. "Can I get out of here now?"

"I'll get an officer to escort you back to your cell. You still have to stay here until ten o'clock."

Bubba shook his head and under his breath was heard to say, "Damn, pigs."

Detective Fenton chuckled. If that was the best the guy could do, he probably was innocent.

Outside the room, in the hallway, Fenton asked the women what was wrong.

Smith answered. "There is something about the passports he's nervous about. Let's ask the guys doing the search of the truck to see if they've found a passport for anyone."

They called the number for the impound yard. When the call was answered, they asked the person if any passports had been found hidden in the truck.

"Funny you should ask that. We just lifted the rug in the sleeping compartment where a corner was loose and found a storage area where about twelve passports were kept. We haven't finished the truck, so didn't call the sheriffs department yet. No drugs were found."

Fenton was excited, "Can you quickly look through them and see if a Maya Toreno or a Maria Hernandez name is on any of them."

"Sure, I've got them right here on the desk and a few cigarette butts, candy wrappers, water and soda bottles."

Fenton snorted. "I don't need a list of things right now. I need to know if any of those passports is for one of these girls so we can hold the truck driver longer."

"Okay, okay, keep your shirt on." There was a lengthy pause. *"Aha, I've got one for Maya Tornado or something."* There was more riffling heard on the phone, *"and I've got one for a Maria Hernandez. That name I can read."*

"Great, check the spelling of Maya's name and read it back to me."

"M-A-Y-A T-O-R-E-N-O."

"Great. Hold those two out for me, but keep the rest handy. This case might be bigger than we thought."

Detective Fenton raised his fist and brought it down fast. "Yes, we've got reason to keep Bubba longer. He had the passports hidden in a storage area in his truck." He shook his head. "Why the hell didn't he get rid of them?"

They rushed to the desk of the jail and informed them of the new evidence.

Almost breathless in their rush, Detective Fenton told the clerk, "Get an officer and tell him to book Earl Bubdecker as a suspect in the disappearance of Maya Toreno and Maria Hernandez. Read him his rights and tell Bubdecker to get a lawyer."

ON AND OFF THE BEAT #24

Laryn went back to her office. She had followed the two detectives as they ran here and there, contacting people she didn't know and with very little communication with her as they went about their business. She felt in the way and was in their way. When she left, they looked relieved and told her they would keep her updated on the case.

She and Officer Brunnell were due in court to testify on the suicide-by-cop and murder case. It was a formality as they had only witnessed the events leading up to the suicide and later cleaned up the mess. Brunnell was on paid administrative leave due to the shooting. Laryn had to testify for Brunnell's right to shoot the victim. Her burses were now gone from the shot fired by the victim, but she had had the required photos taken right after the attack that showed her injuries.

That was one of the things she didn't like about being a police officer. When an event happened, the police officer knew what was going on, but in the court room, you had to convince the judge that what you did was the correct procedure. If there was a jury involved, whew, you had to hope the lawyers gave you the question so you could answer it without looking guilty. What made a person feel guilty just being in the witness stand? Or, Laryn thought, was that just her? She'd ask Farley Brunnell.

As they met up in the hall to the courtroom, Laryn asked Farley that question.

"Farley, why do I feel guilty of a crime by just being here in the courtroom? Do you feel that way?"

Farley laughed harshly. "Hell, Laryn, I am guilty. Right or wrong I did shoot a fellow and I did kill him. I have the nightmares to prove it."

She looked at him, "And I'm glad you did or I wouldn't be here if he'd gotten another shot off. My arm was done for. However, my dreams are of how I might have done things differently. Should I have run a dodge line or crouched?"

Laryn, if you'll remember correctly, we were just catching a speeder. We didn't know he had a gun at that time," he looked sheepishly, "probably shouldn't even be talking about this in case they think we just wanted to get our stories to match."

They waited to be called in to testify. It wasn't a jury trial; it was to prove the killing was justified. There were attorneys for both sides for insurance purposes and family closure.

"Have you had your meeting with the Review Board yet?" asked Laryn.

"Yeah. I think it went okay, but I thought they wanted to talk to you, too?"

"I've seen a note on my desk about that, but I haven't been available to attend yet. Maybe tomorrow if they get together. They know were getting back to normal after the Skagit River Bridge episode."

Farley chuckled. "I missed that because of the suspension. I, also, missed out on all that overtime pay, too. I am enjoying the forced vacation with all this nice weather. My kids are getting to know me," he chuckled again, "and my wife is going crazy with me underfoot all the time. However, I'm getting a lot of repairs done on the house. My wife appreciates that."

They were called into the court room one at a time. As Farley came out, he mouthed "piece of cake' at Laryn. The questions were routine and Laryn left the court room to go back to work.

It had been a busy two weeks for Laryn. She'd had Sunday dinner with her folks. Quinn had come by her apartment a couple of times, bringing rented old movies and something to snack on. She had Quinn to dinner where she had potato salad and chicken hot dogs. Both decided they would never have them again just for health's sake. A hot dog was just that, a hot dog. They had apple crisp with French vanilla yogurt ice cream.

Quinn didn't complain.

She'd had a shift change and was back on the day shift which she liked. She got the call she'd been waiting for. The detectives wanted to talk with her. She went to their office. All the information was there.

Jasper Fenton met her at the door to their office. "Come in Officer Scott." He nodded her in. "May I call you Laryn like Trudie does?"

Laryn nodded, "Yes, please do. It will be easier to talk together if we can just go to first names." They could have called her anything if that made them get to telling her what they knew.

"We talked to Bubba about all the passports. He just told us he kept them for safe keeping for the girls. Since they didn't come back in time to leave Mexico, they were still in his possession. When we asked him how he thought they would get out of Mexico without them, he answered he 'thought' they could contact to the American Consulate."

Laryn shook her head. "The dirty rat! Anything could have happened to those girls that he just left on their own in a town and in a country that isn't really their own anymore."

Trudie nodded, "We mentioned that to him and he said they could be staying with people who would take care of them."

"How did he know that?" Laryn had raised her voice, but calmed down when she heard her own voice echo in the room.

Jasper answered her. "We questioned him about that. He stuttered and hemmed and hawed and finally said that many rich people wanted girls who could speak English and Spanish and would pay them well to teach their kids. He insists that they could have gotten jobs like that."

Laryn squinted her brow in thought. "That's a clue, but how will we find any of these people?"

"Well, we went over everything in his truck and didn't find a clue," shrugged Trudie.

"How about on his person? If he had another girl with him, he might have had a contact for her trip to Mexico."

Jasper's eyes lit up. "Could be! Let's go to Holding and look through his personal effects. He'd have had to eat the darn address if he didn't want it found. Let's get going. He could get out on bond at any minute. We're lucky he hasn't bonded out by now even."

The detectives grabbed their cell phones and a few other things they thought they might need.

Laryn said, "I'll follow you in the patrol car."

At Holding, they asked to see Bubba's personal effects. They were led to a room with drawers. An officer stood over the table as they removed the articles from the drawer. There would be no slight-of-hand removal in this officer's jurisdiction. In Bubba's wallet under a flap that made it hard to find, they found a piece of paper. It just had two telephone numbers on it, one of which looked foreign to them. They wrote down the two numbers and showed the officer that they had returned the note paper back into the wallet. All Bubba's credit cards were in order.

They knew his passport had been in his truck along with all his permits. He looked like an up-and-up guy. He just had too many Latina girls over a period of time unaccounted for.

They returned Bubba's personal effects back to the guard. He thanked them as they were signing out. They saw that they left just in time as Bubba had just bonded out. The officer would have to give him all the stuff in the drawer.

Bubba snarled, "I'm going to sue you all for the interruption of my job and all the money I lost while I was in here."

The officer, who heard this daily, advised him, "Please don't leave the state while this investigation is going on. You're still guilty until proven innocent."

Rather prudently, Bubba kept quiet and stomped out of the building. His truck was still in impound, but he was on his way to getting it back. The detectives and Laryn wondered if he knew all the passports were missing out of it.

They went back to their county office. Laryn followed. She didn't want to miss any of the follow up. In the office, they discussed what to do next.

Trudie spoke, "I think we should call the local number first and see what that is all about. It shouldn't have been hidden if it was on the up-and-up."

"I'll call it. I sound more professional than you women do."

Both women put their hands on their hips and scowled at him.

One woman was fine, but two were intimidating even to an officer of the law. "Okay, I'm wrong in saying that. I just thought I would use my authoritive voice and maybe get an answer rather than you women using your nice voice."

Trudie chuckled, "Good save, Jasper. Go ahead and let's see what comes of the call."

"Let's give this some thought. Shall I say I'm Earl Bubdecker to get the information we need or will that be called entrapment if this goes to trial for unlawful purposes of some kind?"

Laryn thought a moment. "You're right. If they want girls brought back from Mexico for some reason, this is the end that might be more of a reason for prosecution than just Maya and Maria not coming back from Mexico. The Mexican authorities might not care about them anyway."

Trudie intervened, "But we'll never know what this end is all about if we don't call the number."

"In my case, I just want Maya and Maria back. To me it would be enough to just stop Bubba's trafficking of girls." Laryn shrugged her shoulders. "Do what you want to do."

Trudie spoke softly, "How about Laryn and I leaving the room as you call the local number. That way we know of the number, but not who is being called. It might work for us not knowing at this time. If we don't call, the case just might fall through the cracks and die from lack of evidence." She shrugged looking at each person. "After that we'll follow Jasper's lead."

Laryn headed for the door. "That works for me." On the other side of the door, Laryn looked at Trudie with doubt in her eyes. "Do you think it'll work?"

This time Trudie shrugged. "We'll soon find out."

In the other room, Jasper made the call. A male answered the phone. *"Hello, what's the problem?"*

"This is Bubba."

"I told you not to call my private number unless you have the girl."

"I've run into a problem and will be delayed."

"If you can't deliver, I'd like my down payment back and I'll try other sources."

"Hey, I can't give you back the money. I've got a beautiful girl all lined up for you."

"I don't care if she's beautiful or not. Can she understand English and speak Spanish? My daughter wants to learn Spanish and you said the girl would work for room and board. With what I'm paying you, she should work for free, and we'll try to get her citizenship papers started. Now get her here and don't call me on this line again. I'll get another cell phone and call you the new number."

Excitedly, Jasper opened the door and motioned the ladies back in.

Jasper Fenton was astounded and he announced to them. "Bubba was trafficking, but not for sex. He was bringing in chattels, a slave to work for nothing but room and board. It sounded like the girl was to teach Spanish to a spoiled young lady."

"Let's sit down and contemplate what this all means." Trudie pulled out a chair and motioned for the others to do the same.

They sat with their hands crossed on the table and stared at a spot as they adjusted their thoughts to this new information.

Laryn looked up. "Okay, then where are their passports. All Bubba's collection was from the United States, not Mexico, and where does that leave Maya and Maria?"

Trudie spoke, "That leaves them in Mexico without their passport."

Jasper nodded, "Yes, the girls in Mexico have no passports and the girls from there are wet-backs or Bubba brought them here with one, maybe like one of the passports of the girls he took to Mexico."

"God, Jasper, you're a genius." Trudie was excited, "Now let's figure out how this might have worked.

Laryn was amazed at the logic of the two working together. This was fun, if rather serious. "In our view of foreigners, many look alike until you get to know them. With all of Bubba's confiscated passports, he'd have quite a choice."

Jasper nodded, "But wouldn't the Border Guards notice something like that?"

"When I go to Canada, they usually ask me some question about where I'm going and where I was visiting in Canada. I tell them I'm going home to Mount Vernon, Washington and I was visiting Vancouver, Canada. They might ask me if I enjoyed it and do I have any fire arms, drugs, live plants, etcetera, and etcetera." Laryn waved her right hand to add more things. "They punch some keys and I'm on my way."

That said, Trudie added her thoughts. "Bubba could ask a girl if she wanted to go to the United States. They could look over the passports and pick one that looked like the girl. She could memorize the information and be willing to go. Might even be willing to teach a child Spanish just to get in here. She probably wouldn't complain when she gets no pay, only room and board."

Laryn spoke, "I go along with all you've said, but that doesn't explain why we've not heard from Maya and Maria."

"Yeah, but Bubba said they might have gotten a job in Mexico. What if the reverse is true, they're teaching English to some rich, spoiled Mexican kid."

Laryn frowned at Jasper. "But why wouldn't the girls contact their parents and let them know they are working in Mexico?"

Trudie nodded, "Some of those ranches in Mexico are huge. They could be miles from the nearest village and even the village might be miles from anywhere."

Laryn contemplated, "True. Mr. Toreno said his relatives were too far away for Maya to get there. He could only write to them to ask if they had heard from her."

Jasper grabbed a note book and opened to a blank page. "Okay, let's reiterate what we've discussed. "Laryn says Maya's relatives are too far out to get anything but a letter to them. Trudie thinks that some of the ranches in Mexico are huge and far out in the boonies. If a girl was taken out to one to even teach English, she wouldn't have any way to get a message to her relatives in the States or even in Mexico."

Trudie was excited. "Turn to another page, Jasper. We'll start a trip for Bubba.

First he gets a girl who speaks Spanish and fluent English. He's willing to take her to Disneyland, but she must have a passport if she wants to go to Mexico."

Laryn giggled as poor Jasper was writing like crazy.

Unperturbed by Jasper's frantic scribbling, Trudie continued. "Second, he takes them to Mexico and holds their passport for them for safe keeping he says. He must have someone lined up to come and get the girls before-hand, otherwise these girls are smart enough to ask the Border Patrol or even a policeman for help if stranded there."

Jasper raised the pencil in his hand, moving it back and forth to stop the conversation. "Remember, we have another telephone number that is for a foreign country. That might be for our girl Bubba had with him this time, to drop her off for a pickup."

Both women nodded.

"Good point, Jasper," said Trudie.

They kept writing down all the points they had contemplated until they had a fine line on what might have happened with Bubba and the girls he picked up. They looked up from the notes they had just compiled. It was getting late. All three had stayed past their working time so as not to lose their train of thought while they were on a roll.

Now, Jasper smirked, "Okay, now what do we do with all this information?"

Laryn shook her head. "I'm too tired to think right now. The ball has always been in your ballpark. I'm just glad you let me help with this part of it."

Trudie laid her hand on Laryn's. "We were glad for your input. Thanks, Laryn."

Since they were all so mentally tired, they decided to sleep on the problem. They each took a copy of Jasper's information to study and went home to rest.

ON AND OFF THE BEAT #25

Laryn woke to the screaming of emergency vehicles. Since this was a common occurrence in downtown Mount Vernon, she didn't hurry in getting ready for work. If she got a call, she would scramble, but was so tired, she felt like calling in sick. What would happen if Detectives Fenton and Smith called for her? That thought made her speed up in getting dressed.

She'd pick up her coffee on the way to work. She supposed she had better pick up a quick breakfast, too, or Quinn would somehow know she hadn't eaten and rag on her. It was strange how Quinn kept her on a health kick, when he really didn't interfere with her life style. He was just subconsciously there in her mind.

What if he was here all the time keeping her in line and her body in shape? A morning kiss wouldn't go awry either. Was she up to 'Sex in the City' or would both their consciences bother them with Quinn being so close to her family. She knew her Mother would be disappointed in her if they moved in together without a commitment to a lifetime together. Her Dad would have a fit. Even Dayne might have something to say about it. He wouldn't want to lose Quinn as a friend and a mentor to his team if Laryn had a falling out later with Quinn.

She banged her fist to her forehead. Get your head on straight and get to work, she admonished herself. Save Quinn for another time when she had more time to analyze her situation. After all, he'd never said anything about them moving in together or even going steady like the kids did in high school. He just was paying more attention to her lately.

At her workdesk, she drank her coffee and ate a breakfast sandwich she had picked up at the same time. With her free hand she went over her schedule for the week and read bulletins meant to keep them informed of what was going on between debriefings.

Sergeant Diller called her into his office. "I'd like a first hand report on your unofficial case about the Torenos."

Laryn nodded, "Just a minute while I get my report we worked up."

She rushed to her desk and brought the paper back to her boss's office. She handed it to Sergeant Diller.

He looked it over. "I'm impressed. This really makes a case to have Earl Bubdecker kept in custody for further investigation."

Laryn nodded, "I think so, too. We just didn't know where to go from here last night. Maybe today something might have occurred to the detectives."

Sergeant Diller was a huge man and kept himself in great physical shape. "If I had my way, we'd beat the hell out of him until he squealed like a pig and told us everything he knows." He cocked his eye at her, "But we know that would be police brutality and we can never have that, now can we?"

Laryn could hardly contain a smile, "No sir, we can't."

"Well, I'm proud of your part in the case even if we don't have jurisdiction in it. They wouldn't have gotten very far if you hadn't done a lot of the leg work and on your own time, too."

Laryn saluted the sergeant, "Thank you, sir. I felt I had to do something for a friend. I appreciate your part in letting us do the truck stop check. It really made the case when he had Maria Hernandez with him and she came up missing. It cinched it when they stopped him and he had another Latina girl with him."

"What's your plan now?"

"I don't know, sir. I have to wait until I hear from the detectives on the case. I'll keep you in the loop as I might have to leave the office, if requested."

"Do that. You're dismissed." He went back to studying the papers on his desk.

Laryn went back to her cubicle. Tonight she had to do drive-around door checks. She groaned. Door checks were a pain. You had to get out of the patrol car a million times. If it was down town, you could walk the block and come back to the starting place before moving on.

When the stores were farther apart, which were better targets for break-ins, you had to just get out and check the doors. Both being seen checking doors and the occurrence of patrolling an area were helpful to the store owners and sometimes driving by again in about an hour made the crooks leery of breaking in.

When it was time to leave, Laryn took a positive attitude. If she could prevent a break-in and help a store owner, her time was well spent.

Two days went by without any more information about the Toreno case. When Laryn came in from her patrol with Bay Renaldo, and lived to tell about it, there was a message for her to call Detective Smith. That would be the first thing Laryn did when she came in tomorrow.

Meanwhile there would be about an hour of reports she and Bay would have to write up. He had a petulance for spotting trouble which required him to do a 360 and usually snapping Laryn's neck or plastering her nose to the side window. Most of the time, it just broke up a gathering of people who would rather walk away than speak to an officer of the law. She agreed with the group. She would rather walk away than to speak to Officer Renaldo. He was a big, scary brute of a man. He probably did stop a lot of crime by his actions. She paid her dues by having to write up their actions in triplicate.

Laryn arrived at the station early the next morning. She didn't want to miss the detectives if they called again. Meanwhile, she let Sergeant Diller know she was going to call Detective Smith back. He was as interested in what they had to say as she was. She'd report back to him.

She called Smith. "This is Officer Scott. I'm returning your call."

An excited Trudie Smith answered, *"Laryn, have we got news! You know the log book the trucks keep? Well our investigative team that goes over all that stuff with a fine tooth comb spotted something strange in the log book. They had gone over it before so it was easy to miss the first time. At the end of some days, Bubba had written a number in parenthesis. It could have been a number he needed for the next day. It turns out it was a telephone number of a residence in Mexico. If a number was at the first of the day,* it *was a broker for trafficking, the girls. It either said, 'Here's a number to dump the girl.' or another one just said 'Have you got the girl?' One at the front of his log book just said, 'Need girl.' He must have used a disposable phone or even local phones as we've not found any evidence of him calling any of these numbers."*

"Have you found Maya yet?" asked Laryn. This was exciting, but she must stay on task to keep things moving in the right direction.

"No, but we've contacted the American Consulate at the Embassy in Mexico and reported the girls missing. If we find out where the girls are at, they will help get them home and, hopefully, the Mexican government will help stop the trafficking."

Laryn thought a minute. "Is there any chance that Bubba might help if he knows we know all his dirty little secrets? He might want some leniency if he cooperates."

Trudie answered, *"That's a good idea. It would speed up getting the girls home again and maybe some of the Mexican girls sent back that is if they want to go back to Mexico."*

Detective Fenton came on the extension. *"We'll have to put an A.B.P. out on him. When we get him back in custody, he might let some other information escape in his frustration at getting caught in this trafficking scheme."*

Laryn nodded her agreement even if they couldn't see her. "Call me when you know more."

She went back to the Sergeant Diller's office to report what the detectives had found out on the case.

After Laryn's talk with Sergeant Diller, his thoughts were that Bubba wouldn't know any more than what the detectives had found out. Bubba wouldn't want to dirty his hands by knowing anything about where the girls had gone, just that they were going to be taken care of. Laryn concurred with him.

After work, Laryn hit the Health Club to exercise her muscles a little. It didn't hurt to be able to see Quinn for a few minutes either. She had her gym bag with her and changed into her workout clothes before she hit the machines. Since she hadn't run in quite a few days, she decided that would be the machine for her right now. She started slowly and after a few minutes boosted the speed. Quinn hadn't spotted her yet or else he might not even be around.

The punching bag was next on her agenda. She punched, "Take that, Bubba." Another punch and a rapid repeat, "That's for Maya and Maria, you dirty rat."

"I'm glad I'm not Bubba."

She turned around and met a smiling Quinn.

"When I heard the bag begging for help, I knew that my Laryn was giving somebody hell." Quinn quickly kissed her lips when she turned around. He knew he might get the next punch to his gut at startling her, but it was worth it to feel her soft lips against his. She tasted of salt, coffee and vanilla.

He cocked his head at her. "Where did the vanilla come from?"

"Quinn," she flopped her arms over his shoulder and her fighting gloves brushed the back of his neck. "I had a vanilla milkshake to boost my energy before I came here. I'm sure it was a low-fat one," she smiled a beguiling smile at him.

"Yeah, sure. Come on over and we'll get a bottle of water to cool you down."

They walked over to the huge ice chest used to hold water just for the patrons.

"Sit down a minute and tell me what you've been doing lately."

They sat down on the chairs next to the ice chest.

"Quinn, we've got some more news about Bubba and the girls. The detectives found some telephone numbers in Bubba's log book for numbers in Mexico. In calling them they got very cryptic messages, like 'Need Girl' or 'Drop of point is—', that kind of stuff."

Quinn nodded his head. "Okay, now what are you going to do with the information you've collected?"

Laryn shook her head, "We don't know what to do with it yet. Sergeant Diller said we should get Bubba back and shake him until he squeals like a pig, but he was kidding about the shaking."

They sat there with their hands between their legs and the water bottle dangling from their fingers. Laryn swung hers lightly back and forth. Quinn was thinking. What would be a logical thing to do?

"Would it help to get the Mexican authorities involved? Tell them that American Latina girls were taking jobs away from their Mexican counterparts. That might get them to hunting down the patrons whom might have custody of Maya and Maria."

"Good idea, Quinn. How did you get so smart flexing your muscles all the time?"

He knew she was pulling his chain, but retaliated anyway. "I have a lot of time to think when I'm exercising and flexing my muscles. And exercising increases the blood flow to the brain, you know." He looked at her grinning, "Or maybe you don't know since you've been holed up in the police station and haven't been working out like you should and probably haven't been eating right, either."

He watched her ears turn red. Aha, he'd hit the nail on the head. She hadn't been eating right.

"I've been eating right." He cocked his head at her. "All right, I'm eating on the run, but I did buy a breakfast sandwich as I picked up my coffee and I can eat with one hand and with the other hand fill out paper after paper, list after list, schedule after schedule. Now don't you feel sorry for me?"

"I would if you weren't so beautiful when you look contrite. But I do realize you need some good red-blooded meat to perk your blood up. Go home and put a couple of potatoes in the microwave, fix a salad of mixed lettuces, broccoli and cauliflower and I'll bring a couple of thick juicy steaks to barbecue. How does that sound?"

Wow, she'd do anything he wanted just to have him with her for a few hours. "Sure, Quinn, that sounds wonderful. I don't need any more brain exercise. I just need some good red meat, huh!"

She winked at him as she left to gather her clothes and her sports bag to run home and start all the preparations for a dinner with Quinn at her place. Maybe she'd pick up some potpourri to take the stale smell out of the place and wash her slime-ridden fish bowl clean.

ON AND OFF THE BEAT #26

Quinn showed up at her doorstep around nine-forty that night. He must have run to the store and then gone straight there. He also must have showered at the Health Club in order to get there this early. As he entered he kissed her lips again. He was getting good at this sneak attack on stealing kisses as he made a beeline past her straight to her kitchen area. What would it be like if he really laid one on her, she wondered? She'd bet it would be great.

Closing the door, she followed his clean fresh soap smell. Out on her small deck, he started her electric grill. Within minutes he had their steaks grilling. They sat in the small space allotted for two plastic deck chairs. Laryn handed him a wine glass half full of burgundy wine to go with the steaks. They could watch the bend in the river from here. The sun was setting making it reflect the reds of the sunset. Cirrus clouds were painted purple slowly turning to darkness.

When the steaks were done, Quinn took them indoors to eat at her table. The magic moment was gone on the deck and only the bats were flying around.

Quinn looked around her apartment while he ate. This was so homey. He enjoyed the quiet and peacefulness Laryn brought to her home. He'd like to share this kind of time with her. Would she and her family approve if he made an outrageous suggestion to her? It was time to fish or cut bait. Jealousy raged when she brought other fellows to her family's home. It would be hard, but he could skip those Sunday dinners if she didn't approve.

Nonchalantly, he glanced over at her. No need for her to know his knees were knocking beneath the table. "Laryn, would you go steady with me or marry me if I asked you?"

Glancing back at his plate, he stabbed another piece of meat and looked back up at her. Her mouth was hanging open.

"What?" she uttered.

He put his fork down. "Will you marry me and share this peaceful place with me?"

"Why?" She looked confused.

"Well, girl, I find myself jealous of those yahoos you bring to your parent's house. I enjoy your company. I've thought about kissing you until we're both out of our minds, but then I'd want to take you to your bedroom and make love to you. So even though I don't know much about family life, I do know that your family would beat me to a pulp if I did anything like that. Besides, I love everything about you, so that must mean I love you."

"Love?" She looked startled.

He chuckled, "You can't say anything but one word replies?"

From her small retro table she reached over and hugged him, her wine glass wobbling from the jousling. "Yes."

"Yes, you can't say anything but one word replies or yes, you'll marry me and put me out of my misery."

She kissed his cheek and looking into his eyes she replied, "Yes, I'll marry you and put both of us out of our misery." She slowly slid back to her seat as her hands took his where they rested on the table. "You are the only one I want to talk to when I have a problem or even when I'm happy about something. My folks think you're a good guy and my brother would kick me out of the family before he'd give you up. I guess I'm stuck with you or I'll lose my family, too. Yes, my handsome hunk, I'll marry you."

He grinned, a silly grin. "Good, let's chuck the dishes and go to bed now."

Laryn giggled. "I'm afraid there is more to it than going to bed. First you have to sweet-talk my Dad, while I sweet-talk my Mother. I'll have to get birth control pills and we both will need a medical check-up. Where shall we live? Will I work after we get married? I think we have to talk about some things before we commit to this, Quinn. We're not teenagers anymore. We're adults now." She winked at him "Worse luck!"

Quinn looked sheepishly at her. "Okay, scratch going to bed, let's ditch the dishes and go neck on the couch while we discuss these issues."

A quick kiss on his check, she pushed back from the table. "I'm all for that. Lead on McDuff." As she danced around the table with her arms waving over her head, she chanted, "I'm engaged! I'm engaged!"

Back at work, Laryn found there was an A.P.B. put out on Bubba. He was being accused of trafficking girls to Mexico for chattels on both sides of the border. The Mexican Embassy was going to track down the Latena girls who were in their country illegally while working with the American

Embassy in getting the Mexican girls back to their own country if they were willing to go back.

Laryn pondered that message. Would the Mexican girls want to go back or would they just be deported? They could probably get a visa if they wanted to work, but that would put those people, who bought the girls, in danger of being accused of illegal something or other. She didn't know the legal ramifications of all this stuff. Snickering to herself, she thought: if I knew all that, I'd be the lawyer for the girls.

Laryn was called to Sergeant Diller's office. He wanted an update on all that was going on. He knew plenty, but wanted to confirm each detail so that they would be on the same page in dealing with the case that was really out of their jurisdiction.

"I don't want to appear with egg on my face if anyone questions me."

He said that to Laryn's face.

"I understand, sir," was her reply.

"We're on the outside looking in, but it is a damned good case to be familiar with. It would have been just a matter of time before a Latina girl would have disappeared in our area of jurisdiction and how do we know that one of the girls from Mexico isn't right here in Mount Vernon?"

"Good question, sir. If it had been Estelle Baronia instead of Maya Toreno on my phone, it would have been in our jurisdiction. I'm glad we have the detectives on the case to let us off the hook in finding agencies to help with this case and you're right that one of the girls could be right here in our town."

Laryn could see the sergeant puff out his chest. "I'm sure we could have found all the agencies and contacts those detectives found, but it does make it easier to work with them on the case than being on our own, plus costs the city less. You've even done most of your investigation on your own time. Even when I let you go with them, it's been to the jail which is right here in town. Good work Officer Scott. Dismissed." He started moving papers around on his desk.

Laryn shook her head as she left. Dismissed seemed to mean you started moving papers around on your desk, not shake your hand or pat you on the back. She could live with that and she started to smile while she made her way back to her cube where her desk was located.

It was two days before Bubba was apprehended. He had another load, but had no one with him. He had either learned his lesson or was playing it cool. The detectives told her this as they called to see if she wanted to sit in on the interrogation. This time it wouldn't just be a question and answer session but a, *'read-him-his-rights'* and bring out the big guns.

"Yes, I'll be there. Where and when?" Laryn quivered with delight. She still hadn't contacted Mr. Toreno to let him know Maya might be found. She didn't want to get his hopes up and then have them shattered if she wasn't found. Laryn was sure he'd just die on the spot with a second disappointment.

"Tomorrow morning at eight o'clock we'll start. There will be more than just the three of us there questioning him. In fact, we may have to step back and let the government get involved. He crossed the border and that makes it an international case." Detective Smith sounded as disappointed as Laryn felt.

"Bummer," was all Laryn said as she hung up.

Now she had to let the sergeant know and maybe at that point she would be out of the picture entirely. With trepidation, she went and rapped on his door. When she entered, he was still shuffling paper.

As he looked up at Laryn, he mumbled, "Paper work just keeps piling up."

"I'm reporting the newest information about Bubba, sir."

"They caught him?"

"Yes, sir, they did and he didn't have anyone with him this time. He had a load of stuff to deliver somewhere. I wonder what will happen to that shipment?"

"They'll contact whoever it belongs to and they will come and pick it up. They'll be pissed off, but that isn't our problem or the county's."

"Good to know, sir. May I go sit in on the interrogation of Bubba?"

"Sure you can. You've been involved from the beginning, but I'm going, too. When he goes to trial, we all might be called to the stand. I don't want him to get off with a technicality. Our stories have to match, even though I am far out of the loop and I'd tell the court that, too."

"Okay then, I'll see you over at the court house at eight o'clock in the morning, sir."

The sergeant went back to sorting his papers. Laryn presumed she was dismissed.

Back at her desk, she prepared some questions she wanted answered. These questions might be asked by someone else, but that was okay just as long as she got the answers she wanted to hear.

Laryn slept fitfully. Questions kept replicating over and over again. When it was daylight, she gave up and decided a good run would clear her head. It seemed to be touch-'n-go on her runs as to whether or not she'd see something that would cause her to call for back-up. She'd have to ask the other guys if they ran into trouble when off duty. Okay, maybe Bay did, as he seemed to look for it and usually found trouble, at least when she was on duty with him.

With all her busy thoughts, she arrived back at her apartment in record time. She'd have to tell Quinn what a good girl she was and maybe get a kiss for her troubles.

Laryn showered and dressed for a day at court. She had made sure her uniform was a freshly pressed and the shirt was straight from the cleaners. She wouldn't have her gun or accessories on. They were a pain going through the metal detector and not needed in court.

She'd even thought about wearing regular clothes, but decided her message to the court was that she was a police officer, so dressed with that in mind. She touched up her bangs with the curling iron. With or without her hat, she looked like a boy and that wasn't the message she wanted to present either. Finally, it was time to go to the court house. Her day had begun.

Bubba's questioning was over. As far as Laryn was concerned, he had told the truth. Until they found one girl or another, they wouldn't know if they were sold for sex or, just as he had said, for teaching children how to speak English or Spanish. Laryn certainly hoped Maya and Maria were teaching Spanish.

There was hope in finding a Latina girl in Seattle. Bubba didn't often have a load that went there, but his contact was at the Pike Street Market where supplies were given to the vender that had ordered them. It usually was a different person each time that picked up the girl from Mexico.

His only contact with them was a telephone number. He'd call the number when he got a girl for them. That number was never used again after he delivered the girl. He also never used the phone he had again either. The broker he called to get a girl for either Mexico or the United States changed often. He had about ten different numbers so if one didn't work, another one might.

He admitted he got paid money for the girls when one was picked up. The money varied and, yes, the girls worked for nothing. It was Bubba's understanding, that they worked until the family decided they had worked their procurement off, then they would be paid wages for their work.

Bubba didn't know how long that would take or where the girls went after they were no longer needed. He thought maybe they just stayed on as maids. After all, it was a job wasn't it? He did know that those Mexican girls he brought up here were promised a visa or work towards getting immigration status. He thought he was doing those girls a favor.

Laryn was disappointed he knew so little about the girls he dropped off in Mexico. It was like he dropped the girls off to go shopping and then they were abducted. He just didn't know what happened to those girls, but he was adamant they weren't sold for sex, just to teach children the English language.

Laryn and Sergeant Diller discussed the case and questioned each other when a point wasn't clear.

They were unsure how the case about the dead girl would go. Bubba said he was scared when she died on him and he didn't know why. He was almost relieved when they told him she had died from a diabetic coma.

He buried her under that load of alfalfa only because he didn't know what to do. Maya had tripped and hit her head on the stove. She had been afraid of him because he was so mad at her for calling that number he had given her. It had been a joke on a guy, but it backfired as the guy's wife was as mad at him as he had been at Maya. He'd thought he had two dead girls on his hands. He had panicked.

Maya had forgiven him when she came to from the blow on the head and knew she was on her way to Disneyland. Bubba said he had been extra nice to her and had bought her a new wardrobe as he had thrown hers under the alfalfa pile. He didn't know why. He'd been so scared he didn't know what he was doing.

Discussing each point to death, Laryn and Sergeant Diller had decided before hand that they did not want Bubba to get off on a technicality if they were subpoenaed. Laryn only wished he had known more about Maya and Maria.

It was now up to the different countries to work their magic and get each girl involved back to their rightful country.

Now that their notes matched, Laryn was dismissed to go back to her area to do her paper work. Work, work, work, always work. Laryn liked her job, but at times the follow-up on a case was a pain. She felt she'd be better off out on the street fighting crime than just writing about what happened while she was on duty.

The bright spot was she could tell Quinn about her day. What she knew would also be in the newspaper or a version at least, of the case about Bubba.

ON AND OFF THE BEAT #27

Excited about the day she'd had, Laryn called Quinn on her cell phone. He answered, but from the background sounds, he was busy.

"Quinn, when you get off duty, let's go someplace and have a drink and I'll tell you about my day."

"Sure. Okay. Where?"

Taken back a little from his abrupt reply, she could only think Mexican. "How about that Mexican place down by your club? About nine forty-five, okay?"

"Sure. See ya." And he tapped off.

Laryn looked at her phone and shook her head. She shouldn't have called him at work. She knew how busy the club got at times and he had very little help.

At home she changed into nice pair of jeans and a disco sweater. She supposed it was disco as it hung off one shoulder and showed a bra strap. This bra was a Victoria's Secrete bra that matched the color of the sweater. She didn't own very many colored bras, but had bought this one so she wouldn't look sluttish. Her mother would have had a fit if she looked slutty, but then again she had a good thought that her sweater just might end up in another of her mother's books.

In reading the many books her mother had written, she recognized outfits she had worn, plus some her mother wore. She guessed in writing, you wrote what you knew or saw.

At nine forty-five on the dot, Quinn entered the restaurant that had the quaint smell of garlic and tomato sauce. His mouth watered at the smell and his stomach growled. He needed to eat and to heck with healthy non-fat status.

He saw Laryn and quickly went in that direction. At the table he gave her a quick kiss on the lips as her face was looking at him and presented a perfect opportunity.

"Hi, pretty lady. May I sit at your table and partake of your pretty face as I eat?"

"You may, kind sir, if you don't eat me. I'm kind of stringy to eat."

Quinn sat down and grabbed her hand and leaned forward. "I'd love to chew on you, but I do need to eat something first. My stomach growled as I came in and that isn't very romantic. How about a margarita first?"

Laryn grinned. "I've already ordered one for each of us. Nothing fancy, just salt-on-the-edge and slushy."

"Sounds good to me. Now how did your day go with Bubba?"

Laryn's face lit up like a neon sign. "Oh, Quinn, it was great. Bubba sang like a canary. That's police talk and it sounds silly. He spilled his guts sounds more like police talk."

"Laryn, dear, get to the point. I don't care how the police talk, unless it's you spilling sweet-talk into my ear."

Laryn put her hands together as if in prayer and leaned into the table. "He told us all about his operation and how it works. He really didn't know what happened to the girls after he dropped them off at the meeting place. He inferred the girls he brought into the United States knew they were coming up here to a job teaching Spanish to children. The girls he took to Mexico only knew he was taking them to Disneyland and on into Mexico if they wanted to go and that was why they had passports with them."

Quinn cocked his head. "So he doesn't know where the girls are in Mexico?"

"That's right, although, the Mexican authorities are working on the telephone numbers they found in Bubba's log book. We're hoping Maya and Maria will soon be located and brought home. I can hardly wait to tell Mr. Toreno that Maya has been found. Maria's parents have been in touch with us already and have pushed the government to get her home. This helps Maya, too."

Their margaritas were brought to their table and both Quinn and Laryn tasted the refreshing drink.

Quinn groaned in appreciation. "Man that tastes good after a hard day at work." He looked at Laryn. "You're a good friend to have, Laryn. You are like a dog with a bone and will protect it until all harm has passed. You've done more on this case than the rest will ever know."

She blushed and lowered her head. "You're right, but I've only done what a good friend would do. Even though Maya wasn't really my best friend, I did know her and she did call for help. I think anyone in my shoes would do the same."

The waitress came to take their order. They ordered a mixed plate of Mexican food with a glass of tomato juice to cool it down. The juice was healthy, they joked.

"Well, how was your day, Quinn? You've listened to me and all my excitement, but you came in tired, so I know it must have been a busy one."

"It was, Laryn. My helper, Tom, had another heart attack. He came out of it just fine, if you can come out of one of those things fine, but he won't be back for awhile. I'm interviewing for another helper and, hopefully, an older fellow so that the elder group that comes in for exercising and camaraderie will still feel at home there." He grinned, "They tell war stories and sometimes I think its bull stories as they get quite rowdy and loud."

Laryn laughed, "That's so cute."

Quinn frowned, "You'd think cute it you had to handle them and make sure they don't have a heart attack on your shift and keep them hydrated and make sure they work on different machine to get a good work out. Those guys think they've exercised just coming into the gym. I make sure they get on a machine and tell them to get those legs moving. Then I check the rest of the patrons and come back and harangue those guys again. Tom didn't have to leave them to help other patrons and had a routine set up. Those old guys just moved from machine to machine without much instruction. Without their captain, they are a boat without a rudder."

Their food came and they ate hardy. Both were hungry from their long day at work. Both thought the food was wonderfully soothing even if the tomato juice had to quell the heat of jalapeños. They finished off their meal with another margarita and a sopaipilla apiece. Now relaxed, they sat holding hands and listened to a Mariachi band play a few songs, then left, reluctantly, to go to their respective homes.

At home, Laryn reflected on the good-night kiss Quinn had given her out by her car. In such a relaxed mood as both of them had been in, she felt lucky to have gotten away before she had suggested a better way to spend the rest of the night. It wouldn't do Quinn or herself any good to get ahead of their relationship.

In their mind, they were engaged to be married, but in real life, Quinn still had to see her family and she had to talk to her mother about the affair. Her mother thought she and Quinn were just good friends with a strong feeling for each other.

Now that the Maya case-file was coming to an end and hopefully a good end, she and Quinn could invite themselves to another Sunday dinner and inform the family of their new relationship.

It was almost too new for Laryn herself. Quinn was younger than she was, but his experiences made him seem older and very mature. He was shorter, but certainly in good shape, which seemed to make him appear taller. His good looks took away the breath of most women and his athletic abilities made most men like him. Her family liked him.

Okay! He was perfect and Laryn wondered how she had ever caught the eye of such a man.

Quinn walked back to his small apartment near the club. He wondered if his feet even touch the ground. He was madly in love. He figured it was love, because he wanted to be around Laryn all the time. He hated having her out of his sight and it had nothing to do with jealousy. Just being able to look across a room and see her and the graceful way she moved made his heart race. Even on police duty she had a grace she didn't realize she had.

He'd never been one for flirting and talking about the attributes of women with the other fellows, so grace and athletic abilities won over striking beauty and the flirty nature of other women.

Maybe, they could set up another Sunday dinner with her folks and get this engagement underway.

ON AND OFF THE BEAT #28

Laryn called her Mother to see if Sunday dinner was still in the making. She had missed so many that her Mother might not even be having them unless she knew someone was coming to dinner. My Lord, they could even be on vacation for all she knew, but in her heart she knew her Mother would inform her if they were leaving town.

After all, Laryn had to report in if she was leaving town or listen to a tirade about never being found again if she went missing. After all, her Mother listened to the Seattle news and knew about these things. Yada, yada, yada. Laryn's police training meant nothing to her Mother when she went on these benders.

"Hi, Mom. This is Laryn checking in."

"I know who you are, but I'll admit you could be a stranger. How have you been, sweetie?"

"Busy, very busy, but I have time to come to Sunday dinner if that is still what you do on Sundays."

"Hah! Very funny! I cook Sunday dinner for your Dad and me, even if our children are too busy with their lives to even check in. We've been eating a lot of leftovers lately."

"Sorry, Mom, but I do have news about my Latina girl's case, which I will tell you about on Sunday. Will you make enough food to feed Quinn, also?"

"Oh, I'd love to see Quinn. Now that Dayne's kids are through with their sports for the year, we haven't seen Qwinn. I'm wondering if Dayne has a girlfriend as he doesn't seem to be home much either. Has he confided in you, Laryn? Something is going on with my children and I'd sure like to know what it is."

Laryn tried to interrupt her Mother's tirade, but it was hard to stop it once she got going.

"Mom, Mom. When I get there we can discuss it and if Dayne is there we can gang up on him until he surrenders. I can hardly wait to hear him squeal like a pig."

"Laryn, that doesn't sound very nice. We should respect each other's space. Now no more of that disrespect, you hear me."

"Sorry, Mom, I just went on a tirade and couldn't control myself." Hah! She thought to herself. Who started this discussion?

"Come with an appetite, dear. See you Sunday."

"Good-bye for now, Mom. Tell Dad I called."

Sunday finally arrived. Laryn had called Quinn to invite him. She had been surprised to find out he was trying to get Dayne to invite him, also, and was going to call her when he had an invitation. He said he had felt it was too forward of him to ask Laryn to set up a date for Sunday dinner.

He hadn't talked to Dayne either, when Laryn said her Mother had told her, he wasn't around much anymore except to sleep and wash his clothes.

"I wonder what's up?" Quinn asked.

Laryn laughed, "That's what we're all going to find out when we put him on the hot-seat."

"You're evil, girl. Leave the poor guy alone. I know how it feels when you're not ready to tell all."

"Poor baby, should I kiss it and make it better?"

"Ah, you are so lucky that I'm not there or, yes, I'd make you kiss it and make it better right on my hot-to-trot mouth"

She laughed hardily, "See you Sunday, lover-boy," and hung up before he could retaliate.

They met at the door to her folk's home. Laryn walked in followed by Quinn. Laryn's Dad, Jordan got up out of his favorite chair and hugged Laryn and shook hands with Quinn.

"Haven't seen you kids for awhile. Hope all is well with you two?"

"Good to see you also, sir." Quinn's ears turned red.

"I'll talk to you later, Dad. Mom's on my list right now to make up for not coming lately to Sunday dinner." She did a backward wave as she headed for the kitchen leaving Quinn with a caught-in-the-headlight look.

Jordan asked, "Let's go sit down and see what's on TV. Now that the Seahawks have won the Vince Lombardi trophy, we could watch the golfing or the Winter Olympics."

"Sir, I'd like to talk to you first."

"Hey, I was Jordan to you before. I'm still the same guy. Call me Jordan."

"Well, Jordan, I'm here to tell you Laryn and I have been seeing each other for awhile."

Jordan chuckled, "Sure, I know that. Hope you kids have had a good time, although when Laryn has time to date, I have no idea."

Grinning, Quinn agreed with him. "You're so right. When she's off duty, she is really tired and when her schedule is not on regular hours, she's sleeping. Our dates have been more like eating together after I get off work, or I've even cooked for her to keep her alive. Now I have to ask you a question."

Jordan leaned forword, "And what would that be?"

Quinn looked at the floor first before looking into Jordan's eyes. "I'd like to ask for your daughter's hand in marriage, sir."

Inside, Jordan was smiling to himself. He and Samantha had discussed this event, should it ever happen. They didn't think either of their kids was smart enough to realize that someone could be a friend and love them, too. It had finally happened. Laryn had found a guy that was a friend and now he loved her.

He decided to look stern. "What does Laryn think of this idea?"

Quinn wiped his hand over his face. "Well, she's the one that said I had to ask you first and she had to sweet-talk her Mother."

Just then there was a yell from the kitchen. "Jordan, Jordan, the kids want to get married."

Jordan stood up just in time for a fireball to plow into his arms that were held out wide. Samantha was wiping her nose onto his shirt as she cried, in joy, presumed Quinn.

"I just found out, too, Sam. Isn't it great?"

Samantha looked up into his eyes. "Yes, it is great," then she glanced at Quinn. "You're going to make such a handsome groom." Then she glanced around the room. "My gosh, there is just so much to do. Come on Laryn, we've got a lot to think about."

Laryn shrugged her shoulders at Quinn and her Father. "So much to do!" And walked back towards the kitchen as if she was on her way to the gallows.

Jordan looked at Quinn. "Do you think Laryn's happy?"

"I think so. Do we still get to eat dinner?"

Jordan nodded, "It just might be a little later than we thought. Well, kid, welcome to the family." He shook Quinn's hand and sat back down and grabbed the remote to the TV. "Well, what shall we watch?"

A half day into the work day, Laryn got a call from Detective Trudie Smith.

"Laryn, you'll be glad to know that Maya Toreno is here in the United States."

There was a pause as Laryn was screaming she was so excited. This brought those within hearing to surround her. Looking at her group, she reiterated, "Maya Toreno is coming home."

Those present just nodded and went back to work. It wasn't their case, but they knew about it.

"When is she coming home?" Laryn said into the phone.

"When I get the details, I'll let you know. You might want to take Mr. Toreno down to the Sea Tac airport to pick her up."

"I sure will and I'll probably have the blessing of my sergeant. Is it safe to call Mr. Toreno, now? I don't want to have him disappointed. His heart just couldn't stand another disappointment."

"I'm sure it is. My sources say she was flown to Los Angeles by Homeland Security and put up in a hotel until they can get a flight home for her. There will be some interrogation to go along with it, but she is coming home to the good old U.S. of A."

"Oh, thank you, thank you. You guys have been a wonder to work with and to have a happy ending is good for all of our morals."

"I didn't get to tell you about Maria Hernandez. She has contacted her family and chose to stay down there for awhile. She was enjoying her job. That family will now have to pay her wages, but were satisfied enough with her work, so didn't complain too loudly, plus they were kind of under the gun, with holding someone against their will. Down there they will get away with it, but up here they wouldn't."

"That's very interesting. I'll call Maria's family to check in with them. I told them I would. Thank you, again."

They hung up.

Laryn put a call in to Maria's family. She got the Mother.

"This is Laryn Scott. I'm calling to see if you've heard from Maria."

"Yes we have, Laryn. Maria is in Mexico living with a family down there. She is teaching English to the children."

"Oh, how nice for Maria. Is she enjoying her stay?"

"Oh my yes. The family lives near the ocean and have beach privileges. They go swimming each day after the English lesson. She's kind of a nanny to the children, so gets to do a lot of family outings with them. I guess she doesn't have much time to herself, but said that might change soon. We're sending her her passport just in case."

"Well, good for her. Thank you for filling me in. I was worried. Good-bye for now."

Laryn sat there at her desk. Most of the ends were filled in on the cases. Only the dead girl out at the Toreno place was unclear. She didn't have to worry about that one as it was out of their jurisdiction, plus sometime there was a case that was never solved. Worse luck for that case. Laryn gave a little prayer for the one at the Toreno place.

Laryn decide to go out to Mr. Toreno's home to give him the good news. It didn't feel right to just call him.

After work she went out there. He was home and just getting his supper. He was surprised to see her, although a little apprehensive. Laryn knew she was either good news or more bad news to him. Being the gentleman he was, he invited her in.

"Could I get you a cup of coffee or tea, Ms Scott?"

"No thank you, sir. You just get your plate filled and we'll talk while you eat."

Feliz filled a plate with his favorite biscuits and put them on the table. He then filled his dinner plate and returned to the table.

"Please have a biscuit, Miz Scott. I can't eat in front of you." Feliz looked so downcast, Laryn complied.

"Mr. Toreno, I have good news for you."

Feliz looked up. He still wasn't sure he should feel anything. Laryn could tell by the way he glanced up and then back to his plate.

"Your Maya has been found alive and well in Mexico. She is in Los Angeles right now and should be on her way home as soon as they get reservations for her."

Tears welled up in Feliz's eyes. "Is true?"

"Yes, it is true. When I get the call, I'll take you to Seattle to pick her up. She does need a bus ride to get home so we'll go get her, you and I."

Feliz put his hands together as in prayer. "Madre de Dios!" He looked up at Laryn again. "You will do this for us?"

"Of course I will. I'll call you and arrange a time when I know more. Take care, Mr. Torreno. I must go."

They both left the table. Feliz took Laryn's hand "Gracias me amiga. Gracias."

Laryn nodded and left.

She could hardly wait to tell Quinn all her good news. Maybe she'd stop by the Health Club and work out a little and arrange a time to tell him the news. It wouldn't be time for Quinn to close up when she got there. She wasn't really dressed for the workout, either. But who cared if she smelled of sweat? She'd shower when she got home.

Quinn was busy when she came in. He waved at her and kept on helping the person he was with. She went to a tread machine and started walking. She didn't work hard, just a gentle walk

When Quinn broke free, he came over and gave her a gentle kiss on the cheek as he bent over making like he was checking her machine.

"How ya doing, lovely lady?"

"I'm doing fine and wonder how we can get away from this place, so I can tell you about my day."

He looked harassed. "I can't get off until my usual time. I'm so under-staffed right now." He grinned, a winning grin at her. "You wouldn't want to work for me, would you?"

"I don't think they would let me moonlight here while I'm holding down my policing efforts." She made a woe-is-me face.

He grinned. She could always brighten his day. "My tough luck and the city's gain."

Laryn shrugged, "Okay, love, I'll get us huge take-out salads and fresh shrimp to go on top. Come to my place after work. We'll talk and eat and someday soon, we'll also make love."

Quinn's ears turned red again. Clearly he didn't know how to handle frustration or Laryn, but he could try. "I'll be there with bells on and someday a box of condoms."

Now Laryn's ears turned red. She wasn't used to sex talk any more than he was.

Quinn came to her house just as he said. Laryn let him in. Their bowls of shrimp salad were setting on the retro table ready to eat. Laryn had a glass of white wine by each bowl. He washed his hands in her sink and sat down.

Quinn raised his glass, "Here's to our life together. May it always be as much fun as we've endured lately and more fun when we can do it together."

Laryn chimed in as they clinked their glasses together, "And maybe in a few years I'll quit the force, and come to work for you and we'll face all those old guys together."

They grinned at each other, "Amen to that."

XXXXX
By Robin Wood

I AM A POLICE OFFICER THEREFORE I SERVE AND PROTECT

*POLICE FORCE MOTTO:

USA= *PROTECT and SERVE*

LONDON= *FIDELITY, BRAVERY and INTEGRITY*

SCOTLAND= *ALWAYS VIGILANT*

By Mary Anne Wilson

In

"A Question of Honor"

Edwards Brothers Malloy
Oxnard, CA USA
June 30, 2014